SUNSHINE ON THE MOUNTAINS

by

MARGARET MALCOLM

HARLEQUIN BOOKS

TORONTO
WINNIPEG

Original hard cover edition published in 1972
by Mills & Boon Limited, 17 - 19 Foley Street,
London, W1A 1DR, England

© Margaret Malcolm 1972

SBN 373-01699-9

Harlequin edition published July 1973

Printed in Canada

CHAPTER ONE

ON the whole, the staff at the Tannenhof Hotel decided that their first impressions of Charles Ravenscroft were favourable. He was, of course, one of those who knew what they wanted and would see that he got it, but on the other hand, he would not be unreasonable in his demands and, perhaps most important of all, he would never make unpleasant scenes in public if anything should go wrong. Moreover, his tips, though not lavish, were suitable. One would not receive the colossal tips which the inexperienced could sometimes be browbeaten into giving, but good service would have its reward. That had already been made clear.

News of that sort travels fast, and by the time Charles had unpacked and settled in, he came down from his room to find a smiling waiter on the alert to direct him to the lounge—or perhaps the bar for an aperitif? Yes?

Charles lowered his first drink in a contented frame of mind. He was glad that instead of going to a fashionable hotel in one of the famous winter sports centres he had chosen the little Tannenhof at Alpenglühen. Of course, it wouldn't always be as quiet as this—at the moment he had the bar to himself—because naturally at this time, his fellow guests would be out enjoying themselves. And he looked forward to being out as well. For the moment, he was more than content to enjoy solitude and the comfort of the huge log fire.

He sighed appreciatively. For so long he had been working at top pressure and never more so than in the last year when he had combined his hospital duties with incredible hours of the study he deemed necessary if he was to achieve his ambitions. As a result, though he had taken good care not to let anyone else suspect it, he had been more tired than he cared to admit even to himself when the time came to put all the work he had done to the final, gruelling test. Even when it was all over and the pressure was off, he showed no apparent signs of anxiety, as many men would have done, as to whether or not he would achieve the coveted additional qualification which would influence the whole of his future career. Not that his acquaintances—he had few if any friends—were surprised at that. They said, among themselves, that there was something inhumanly cold-blooded about Charles. Always had been. No use worrying once the die was cast, of course, but you'd expect a chap to show some signs of strain.

Except, of course, it was admitted, Charles would inevitably succeed at anything he tackled and eventually he would get to the top of his particular tree. He would see to that, and no human weakness would be allowed to interfere with his progress. To do so would be condoning a fault which he would not tolerate in himself and with which, incidentally, he had no patience when he came across it in others.

None the less, when he heard the news of his success, he did something so apparently out of character that no one who knew him could believe their ears. He decided to take a holiday.

Actually, it was a thoroughly practical and well thought out move. No one knew better than Charles that good health is an essential prerequisite of an ambitious man. And, reluctantly, he had had to confess that he was tired. Tired to such a degree that sleep was far too often elusive, and when it did come, did not give the refreshment it ought to. He prescribed for himself the same treatment that he would have advised a patient. Complete relaxation in conditions where no one could make professional calls on his time and brains, plenty of fresh air and exercise. In other words, a holiday.

And it all fitted in so well. Though it wasn't official yet, he had heard confidentially from a very reliable source that with the new qualification to his credit there would, practically without doubt, be the offer of an appointment at Queen Caroline's which would itself be a springboard for still further advancement.

If there was a drawback it was that the offer would

not be made for a couple of months. But was that really a drawback? Wasn't providential a better description? Not only would a request for a longish holiday—say a month or six weeks—be reasonable since he had taken no time off for the last eighteen months, but since, during that time, he had been so busy one way and another that he had had no time to spend money on anything but the most basic of needs. He could afford a holiday without encroaching one penny on his precious capital.

At first he had found it difficult to decide where he would go. In search of sunshine, since this was winter—and a particularly nasty one? The Bahamas, perhaps. Or a cruise southwards? He turned both ideas down. Either, he felt, would mean meeting more people than he relished and, in the case of the cruise, one would not be able to escape them. Besides, too much sunshine could be enervating. What he wanted was the bracing effects of fresh air and exercise. So, finally—Alpenglühen.

And now that he was here, first impressions confirmed the wisdom of his choice. Here, if anywhere, he should be able to find renewed health and vigour—always providing, of course, that his fellow guests were reasonably congenial and undemanding.

They were beginning to drift in now, chattering and laughing, a jolly-looking crowd of mixed nationalities but alike in one respect. They were all intent on having a good time and, in holiday mood, were prepared to show friendliness to a newcomer. Well, that suited Charles. He wasn't gregarious by nature, but he was well aware of the danger of getting a name for being anti-social. He would make this an opportunity for polishing up his rather rusty social graces.

Quite a few of the newcomers had gone straight up to their rooms, but he was soon in conversation with half a dozen men and one or two girls who had stopped off at the bar. The men were, perhaps, rather over-hearty, but the girls were undeniably attractive and Charles was no misogynist, even though marriage formed no part of his plans for a good many years to come. It was quite a pleasant interlude, but Charles, having no wish to become involved in a long session, made his escape as soon as he decently could.

It was no more than chance, of course, that he happened to come out into the hall just then, though later, he was to wonder if fate hadn't played some part in it. For at that moment a girl came in from the dazzling sunshine and instantly those other girls in the bar were blotted out of Charles's mind. And yet she had no real pretensions to beauty—or it may have been that Charles wasn't partial to tawny red hair and the alabaster skin that went with it. None the less, she had something—

"Good lord, she's absolutely, incredibly happy!" Charles thought with conviction.

You couldn't miss it. Happiness radiated from her like warmth from a fire, and she could no more restrain it than the fire could restrain its heat.

She glanced curiously at Charles, evidently appreciating that he was a newcomer, and then she smiled, simply, Charles was sure, because she felt a friendliness towards all mankind. Then she ran lightly up the stairs and paused on the balcony formed by the landing at the back of the hall. Her eyes were fixed on the hotel door and she was either unaware or indifferent to the fact that she had an audience, for she made no attempt to hide her anticipation. She was clearly waiting for someone very special to come in.

"The man in the case," Charles diagnosed, and knew that he was right, for at that moment, the girl's face changed. It had been happy before. Now it was utterly enraptured as she raised her hand in a gay salutation. Then she saw Charles and with a little gasp, scurried along the landing and was lost to sight.

Charles turned, curious to see what sort of man it was who could bring a look like that to a girl's face. Somebody pretty marvellous, he imagined. A girl like that would surely set a high standard—

Involuntarily he gave a startled exclamation. Well-built, blond hair and beard and deeply blue eyes—the man could pose as a Norse god without the least difficulty. He was, without doubt, the most handsome man Charles had ever seen. But when you had said that, you had said everything in his favour that was possible.

Every doctor needs to be something of a psychologist, and Charles was no exception. None the less, he felt that it should have been patent to anyone with average intelligence that here was the supreme egotist whose only criterion of behaviour was his own comfort and well-being. It showed in the arrogant tilt of the blond head, in the slightly swaggering walk, but above all, in the shrewd eyes and the complacent smile.

And this, Charles thought distastefully, was the man who had brought that radiance to the girl's face! Others might see his faults. To her he was the whole world.

"Little fool!" Charles thought impatiently. "Can't she *see*? She's heading for a fall and when it comes, she'll take it hard. Oh, well—" he shrugged his shoulders. It was no business of his and in any case, if he did try to warn her, she wouldn't believe him. She would probably be furious as well. No, there was nothing he or anyone else could do. He went slowly into the restaurant.

Dinah kept up her headlong retreat until she reached the sanctuary of her own room. She leaned against the closed door, her arms outstretched, flushed and breathless.

She had given herself away completely. The new man had looked at her in quite a sympathetic way— Charles would have been surprised to hear that—but at the same time, she had felt that his dark eyes had probed right into her very heart. Not that it could have been so difficult. Just seeing Nicky made her love for him burgeon like a rose in the sunshine. Almost certainly, that must show in her face.

And after all, what did it matter? They had nothing to hide. Nothing to be ashamed of. She sat down on her bed and gazed unseeingly into the cheval mirror that faced her.

Nicky, Nicky, *wonderful* Nicky! The one person who had ever really loved her—*wanted* her more than

9

anyone else in the whole world! That would mean a lot to any girl. To Dinah Sherwood, it was of supreme importance.

Idly her mind drifted back over the years as it had done so often lately. Somehow the loneliness and neglect of those early days enhanced her present happiness.

She saw herself, rather a plain and far too serious a little person, braving the terrors of an interview with the headmistress of the boarding school which was the nearest thing she had had to a home because she wanted to *know*—had to know.

"Why," she began clearly, "have other girls got homes and parents and brothers and sisters—and I haven't?"

There had been a moment of embarrassed silence. Then Miss Nesbit had hedged.

"Sometimes God doesn't send more than one child to a home."

"Yes," Dinah had agreed, reasonable but persistent. "That, of course, would explain me not having any brothers or sisters. But Joy Turrell is an only child. So is Sheila Brett. But that doesn't stop them from having parents and a home, does it?"

Injudiciously, Miss Nesbit met Dinah's eyes—big, limpid and challenging. Truthful eyes. Looking into them, Miss Nesbit knew that only the truth would satisfy the child.

"Dinah, my dear, you are a sensible little girl and you—you mustn't dwell on this. Your parents were not happy together, so—so—" she hesitated. It was even harder than she had anticipated.

"So they got divorced," Dinah said crudely. "I see."

"Don't judge them too harshly," Miss Nesbit urged gently, shocked at the pain in the child's eyes. "Sometimes people do find that they've made a mistake—you're too young really to understand—"

"I understand enough to know that they were beastly selfish," Dinah retorted bitterly. "Neither of them has ever cared what happens to me."

"Your father provides generously for all your necessities," Miss Nesbit reminded her. "And for luxuries," she added, seeing how little impressed Dinah was.

10

"H'm." Dinah considered that. "What does he do for a living?"

"He's a research chemist—a very brilliant one."

"And where does he live?' continued the relentless cross-examination.

"At present I believe he is in America," Miss Nesbit said shortly, wondering where all this would end.

"I see," Dinah said disparagingly. "Leaves me like luggage not wanted on the voyage and goes off to enjoy being patted on the back for being so brilliant! And my mother?"

"I don't know anything about her," Miss Nesbit admitted truthfully.

"I suppose that means she was the guilty party," Dinah commented to Miss Nesbit's consternation. Really, the things children knew about these days!

"I couldn't say," she said with finality.

"No, of course you can't," Dinah agreed, devastatingly matter-of-fact. "It somehow isn't quite nice to criticise a mother, is it? Well, thank you very much, Miss Nesbit, for explaining. I hope I haven't been too much of a nuisance." She paused, turning over what she had just heard in her mind. "Well, even making allowances, I must say I think I've got perfectly rotten parents! I think I shall have to invent some new ones. So if you hear that my mother is a chronic invalid and my father is an Oxford don who is going blind, you won't contradict it, will you? I'm sorry I have to crock them up like that, but it will explain why they can't come to see their idolised only child and why I don't go home for holidays. You do understand, don't you?"

Miss Nesbit did, and Dinah's friends had to as well. She hid her hurt behind an impenetrable barrier of pride. To pity her was to lose her friendship for ever.

Later, when Dinah was between seventeen and eighteen, there was another interview, but this time it was Miss Nesbit who instigated it. She had news for Dinah. Esmond Sherwood was dead.

Dinah took the news calmly and was not particularly grateful when she learned from the solicitor who came to the school to see her that her father had left her his not inconsiderable fortune.

"Well, so he should," she told the man. "He really owes it to me, don't you think? And if you expect me to cry about it, you'll be unlucky, that's all!"

All that was four years ago now. An interesting four years and quite good fun, really. For one thing, she had somehow outgrown her plainness, which in itself had given her a certain self-confidence. She had left school and had gone to live at the London home of one of the friends she had made there. The Joliffes had treated her like a second daughter. She and Ellen shared a London Season. Together they had been taken to a Garden Party, danced till all hours, taken the theatre, opera and ballet in their stride—in fact, gobbled life in huge, indigestible lumps such as only the very young could survive. And of course, they met a lot of pleasant young men. Ellen, in fact, became engaged to one of them. Dinah didn't. She liked quite a lot of them. They were good fun. But—

"You see," she confided in Ellen, "my parents made a mess of marriage. Well, I'm determined I won't. So I've got to be absolutely, positively *certain* that it's the Real Thing. Do you blame me?"

"No, I don't," Ellen admitted, twiddling her new ring. "You're quite right, of course. One *does* want to be quite sure. *I* am," she sighed ecstatically.

Dinah hesitated.

"Ellen, *why* are you so sure? Oh, I'm not questioning that you are. But *how* did you know?"

"Because it was just like a bomb going off inside me," Ellen explained, more graphic than romantic in her choice of description, but all the more convincing for that. "Just—everything else gets blown into tiny fragments and all that's left is one person who really matters. Oh, you'll know all right, Dinah! You don't need to worry about that!"

And how right she had turned out to be! Dinah thought blissfully. Why, the first moment her eyes and Nicky's had met, something had happened to her. It was as if a brilliant light had been lit in her—her heart had turned over—

And it wasn't long, either, before she knew that Nicky had felt the same thing. That first exquisite kiss—she had said something about the wonder of them both happening to have come to the Tannenhof at the same time.

"Oh, that wasn't *chance*," Nicky had assured her. "That was Fate—capital 'F'! We were *meant* to meet! I knew that the first moment I set eyes on you!"

That had been two weeks ago and now—her dreams were cut short by the loud clangour of the big cow-bell that was used instead of a gong. Heavens, lunch would be served in ten minutes and she hadn't even changed yet!

When she arrived in the restaurant, flushed and breathless, most of the other guests were already at their tables—including the new man. He was facing the door through which she had come and he half rose as she passed his table. Dinah smiled in acknowledgement, but hurried on to her own table. This was situated in a small alcove together with another single table at which Nicky was already seated. He stood up as she slid into her chair.

"You're late, love," he remarked in a gently reproachful way which suggested that every moment he was not with her was so much wasted time. "Nothing wrong, is there?"

"Not a thing," Dinah assured him blithely, surreptitiously slipping her hand into his under the protective shield of the table. "Just—I started day-dreaming. So really, it's all your fault!"

Nicky smiled and gave her hand an answering squeeze. Then, as the meal was served, they discussed various plans for the next two or three days, and it was only as the restaurant was emptying that Nicky asked casually:

"Who's your boy-friend?"

"My boy-friend?" Dinah repeated, puzzled until Nicky jerked his head in Charles's direction as he stood up to leave. "Oh, him! I've no idea. He's new, of course."

13

"Is he?" Nicky asked, frowning slightly. "I got the impression that you knew him."

"Good gracious, no," Dinah denied cheerfully.

"But you smiled at him as if you were old buddies," Nicky accused, the frown deepening.

"Did I?" Dinah laughed and shrugged her shoulders. "Well, I suppose the truth is, I feel like smiling at everybody, these days!" And then, as Nicky's face didn't clear, she added anxiously: "Nicky, you surely didn't think—"

"No, not seriously," Nicky admitted moodily. "It's just that I hate seeing you notice another man, let alone smile at him!"

"But, Nicky—" Dinah protested, on the verge of reminding him that if anyone should be jealous, she was the one, since quite a few of the women did their best to inveigle him to their sides. But one couldn't say that sort of thing so, instead, she said gravely: "There's only one man whom I really see—and you know who that is!"

"Bless you!" Nicky muttered. "But the fact is, I'm so infernally jealous where you're concerned. I can't believe my own luck, you see. After all, why should a wonderful girl like you care two straws for a ne'er-do-well like me? What have I got to give you?"

"Happiness," Dinah told him softly. "The knowledge that I'm wanted—that I'm first in your heart!"

"You're that all right," Nicky assured her. "But it doesn't alter the fact that most people would say I was a rotter ever to have told you that I love you. With a miserable job like mine—"

It wasn't the first time that Nicky had said things like that, and Dinah never knew what to do about it. How could one possibly say: "Well, I've got enough for both of us!" It would be far too damaging to a man's pride—and Nicky *was* proud. She had reason to know that, so she contented herself with saying earnestly:

"Nicky dear, don't call yourself a ne'er-do-well. It does hurt so. And it isn't true. You've had bad luck

14

through no fault of your own, which is something quite different."

"Oh, I grant you, I've had my fair share of that," Nicky agreed morosely. "But other people are unlucky as well, yet they manage to make out just the same. Oh well, there it is! You'll be marrying a poor man, my poppet, and one with precious little in the way of prospects, either. And yet the deuce of it is that, not for the first time, if only I'd got the capital, there's a marvellous opportunity that I could grab. It would be a goldmine, too. Money! What a curse it is when you haven't got it!" he finished bitterly.

And that, surely, was the time to tell him—yet Dinah remained tongue-tied. Afterwards, she was to ask herself why she had felt like that. Partly, of course, because she had full control of only part of her capital. The remainder was in trust until she was twenty-five. Even so, she could realise quite a large sum at once. But that, of course, would reduce her income considerably— something which her father's solicitor had warned her of in no uncertain terms.

"You must remember, Miss Sherwood, that while capital is something which it takes years to accumulate, once you start using it as income, it can vanish almost overnight. So live within the income which your capital produces. After all, that's simply Mr. Micawber's maxim—and he knew what he was talking about, poor shiftless soul that he was!"

But she wouldn't be using capital as income if she financed Nicky's project, whatever it was. She would simply be transferring it from one investment to another. And one, moreover, which Nicky believed would be a goldmine. So since she not only loved but trusted him—

But it was no good. She was too much afraid that Nicky's pride would make him refuse her offer point blank. So she kept her own counsel, comforting herself with the conviction that he would feel different about it once they were married.

All the same, there were times when she felt uneasy. Suppose, when he *did* know, he thought that she hadn't told him before because she hadn't trusted him suffi- ciently? It *could* happen—

She tried to push the thought from her, but obstin- ately, it remained, a shadow which threatened her otherwise perfect happiness.

Within a few days Charles became familiar with his surroundings, and once again he congratulated himself for having chosen to come to Alpenglühen. The place was a little jewel. Its development as a skiing centre was too recent for the village-like character of the little town to have become over-commercialised and the narrow streets with their quaint old chalets and shops were still mainly as they had been when they had originally been built. Some of the chalets, it was true, had been en- larged and were now small hotels, and some of the shops dealt almost exclusively in winter sports outfits and tackle, as well as the inevitable trophies designed to tempt the homegoing visitor. But on the whole, Alpenglühen seemed mildly surprised at its new popu- larity and so far had not seen fit to exploit it to any degree.

Probably it wouldn't be very long, Charles thought regretfully, before the character of the place changed as it became more widely known, but in the meantime he revelled in the peace and tranquillity of the little town which was so dramatically emphasised by the majesty of the mountains which surrounded it.

Once or twice he went to the ski-slopes, but as an onlooker only. He admired the daring of those who, with varying skill, spent every available moment at their chosen pastime, but at the same time he couldn't help feeling that they were fools to risk their necks so recklessly. Still, it suited him very well that most inter- est centred on skiing, for it meant that the beautiful little lake was almost exclusively his, and he had always enjoyed skating, though it was some years since he had had any opportunity of indulging in any. As a result, he had a few initial mishaps, but much of his earlier skill soon returned. And, just as he had hoped, exercise and plenty of fresh air were combining to give him an increasing feeling of well-being. He was sleeping much better, and as for his appetite, it was prodigious, though that was no doubt partly due to the fact that the catering at the Tannenhof was first class. In fact, the standard of the hotel in all respects was good.

It wasn't difficult to know why. Herr and Frau Berger played a very personal role in the running of it, ably assisted by their son, Emil, and his pretty little English wife. Charles took to the young couple to a far greater degree than to any of his fellow guests, partly because their competence added a lot to his comfort, but not a little because of their obvious happiness in one another. Not that they ever flaunted it to an embarrassing degree, but the occasional touching of hands and the quick exchange of a look told their own tale.

It was to Emil that Charles always went if he wanted information and he sought him out one day after having taken a rather longer walk than usual.

"Emil, there's a chalet one can see from the Ski Club —larger than most of them and apparently unoccupied. What is it—a hotel that didn't make out?"

"Oh no." Emil sounded almost shocked. "It is a private residence, the property of an Italian count. He is, however, a busy man and he rarely occupies it at this time of the year."

"He's missing something," Charles commented, and Emil nodded vigorously.

"So I think," he agreed. "But—" with a philosophic shrug, "these days, even the nobility must work like the rest of us if they wish to be prosperous."

"Yes, I suppose so," Charles agreed indifferently, his curiosity satisfied. But Emil, it appeared, had some more information to impart.

"There is, however, a rumour—from what is usually a very reliable sourse—that the Chalet Farini will shortly be opened since the Contessa plans to spend some time there. That is good news, although—" Emil sounded regretful, "it is not likely that we shall see much of her. The poor lady, though not an invalid, does not enjoy very good health."

"Hard luck," Charles commented non-committally,

thanking his stars that he had had the foresight to register as 'Mr.' and not 'Dr.' Ravenscroft. He was, in fact, all the more pleased because there was another doctor staying at the hotel who, far from seeking anonymity, positively advertised his profession by reading—and leaving about—various medical tomes. A bore of the first degree, Charles decided. Too ready to give advice that hadn't been asked for and far, far too prone to tell long stories in which he always featured to advantage. Charles avoided him like the plague, but at least he would probably be only too willing to wait upon a titled patient—which would let Charles himself out. *He* had no wish to be roped in by a hypochondriac, however noble.

The rest of the visitors Charles found pleasant enough if not particularly interesting. There were two or three families with teenage sons and daughters who had linked up to make a self-sufficient little group—Charles never did discover who was related to whom or, indeed, anything much about them except their first names.

There were half a dozen youngsters in their twenties who had come in one party. They were a bit on the noisy side, but so obviously enjoying themselves that one tolerated their high spirits with a shrug, which might, perhaps, hold a certain amount of envy.

And of course, there was the red-headed girl. Her name was Dinah Sherwood and she was here on her own, which was rather surprising. Not that Charles had old-fashioned notions about the necessity of a girl having a chaperone. If this one wanted a holiday on her own—why not? Yet she was surely very young to be of a solitary nature? It would have seemed far more natural to Charles that she, too, should have been one of a group, either family, or one of a party of people about her own age.

Not that she lacked companionship. The Norse god was her constant shadow whenever opportunity offered. And actually, despite his instant prejudice, which had never waned, Charles found the man the most interesting character of them all. His name, it appeared, was Nicky Gisborne and he was the instructor of the Alpenglühen Ski Club. That Charles found surprising, for one would hardly have expected that the modest little club would be able to afford to pay a salary which would be sufficient for their instructor to live at the Tannenhof. Of course, when visitors wanted coaching, no doubt he had quite a good cut of the fees they paid—but even so—

It was only after he had spent a week at the hotel that it occurred to Charles to wonder if, perhaps, the versatile Mr. Gisborne had other sources of income. He was, for instance, a superlatively good bridge player and was frequently in request to make up a four. Charles, himself a sound if conservative performer, watched the play with interest and quickly noticed that despite fluctuations of fortune during the game, it was rarely if ever that Nicky Gisborne was down at the end of the session. Not surprising, perhaps, seeing how high his standard of play was yet all the same, sufficiently disturbing to make Charles resolve not to get involved in any school which also included Nicky. He had no wish to benefit as the man's partner nor to go down as his opponent.

In fact, he had so far not been asked to join in. But visitors were constantly coming and going and a particularly large exodus happened to include most of the enthusiastic bridge players. Nor did the incomers provide a fresh supply since they happened to be family groups who, if they played at all, preferred to make up a four from their own number.

Charles gleaned this information one evening before dinner. Nicky and Dinah came into the bar, and from the moment they arrived, it was clear that they were in disagreement about something. They brought their drinks to a table next to the one at which Charles was sitting and almost immediately Dinah returned to the subject which they had evidently been discussing before.

"Darling, I do understand how much you enjoy playing," she began earnestly. "But after all, you've played almost every evening this week, so wouldn't it be rather fun to have a change? There's sure to be dancing after dinner—and you do enjoy that, too, don't you?"

"Yes, I do," Nicky replied without much enthusiasm. Then, seeing the disappointment in Dinah's face, he added hastily : "At least, I do with *you*. But—" He bit his lip as if he was trying to think of an explanation which would convince her. "You see, Di, bridge is more to me than a pastime. It's—*exercise*. Mental exercise. And with a job like mine, I *need* it, believe me! Without something like that, in next to no time, I'd be no more than a hunk of muscle and brawn—and that would be intolerable !"

And Charles, who had perforce heard every word of the conversation, had to admit that he'd got something there! And yet somehow it wasn't entirely convincing.

It certainly didn't convince Dinah. She sat silent with downcast eyes, slowly twisting her glass on the table top.

"I know what you're thinking," Nicky challenged morosely. "That it's only an excuse—that being a professional skier must mean that one has to have one's wits about one. And that's perfectly true. Otherwise one wouldn't get very far. But—" he shook his head emphatically, "it's not the same as using one's brains for an exclusively mental activity. Surely you can understand that?" he finished with the first hint of impatience that he had shown.

It was a mistake, for it had the effect of making Dinah's firm little chin set obstinately.

"I do understand," she insisted. "And what's more, I sympathise. All the same—" she paused, biting her lip, and Nicky finished the sentence for her.

"All the same, it's not much fun for you! And of course you're right. Well, at least there's no need to argue about it this evening. There's no chance of making up a four, so—" he shrugged, "we dance! That is—" he turned so suddenly, so unexpectedly to Charles that the movement seemed almost to constitute a threat. "Unless *you* will make up a four, Mr. Ravenscroft?"

Charles didn't hesitate. More than ever now he was

determined not to become involved in any of this young man's activities, whatever they might be.

"Thanks, but I'd rather not," he said equably. "It's not my game and—" deliberately he allowed their eyes to clash, "I should certainly spoil yours!"

He heard the hissing intake of Nicky's breath and saw the instant chilling of the blue eyes to diamond hardness.

"And just what do you mean by that, Mr. Ravenscroft?" he asked, his voice dangerously soft.

Charles finished his drink and stood up before he replied.

"Exactly what I said, Mr. Gisborne. I'm an indifferent player and a far from enthusiastic one. Consequently, I couldn't give you a good game." And with a courteous inclination of his head to Dinah—who made no acknowledgement of it—he turned his back on them, returned his glass to the bar and strolled out, conscious that he had left an uneasy silence behind him. Then, as he passed through the swing door, everyone began to talk at once.

But that was not the end of it. Before the day was done Charles came to regret that his determination to avoid involvement with Nicky Gisborne had outbalanced his discretion.

He was just finishing his dessert course at dinner when Emil Berger came to his table.

"Mr. Ravenscroft, it would give my wife and me great pleasure if you will take coffee with us in our own quarters. We can also offer you a brandy which I think you will enjoy."

He was smiling, but Charles was fully aware that this was more than a pleasant invitation. It was in the nature of a request which, given opposition, might well harden into something even less pleasant.

"How kind, Herr Emil," he said composedly. "I shall be delighted. Now?"

"If you please," Emil said with a little bow.

The two men left the restaurant followed by the curious eyes of other diners who, like Charles, had little difficulty in appreciating why the invitation had been given.

But when they reached the Bergers' sitting room, there was no immediate indication that this was anything but an entirely social occasion. Emil's pretty little English wife made him welcome and poured out the coffee while Emil attended to the brandy.

For a time conversation flowed easily on general topics. Then there was a silence which Charles made no attempt to break. He liked the young Bergers, but if they had something special—and possibly unpleasant—to say, they would have to get started without any assistance from him. He waited, saw husband and wife exchange glances and braced himself. So, he fancied, did Emil.

"Mr. Ravenscroft, it has given us great pleasure to have you with us as our personal guest," he began rather as if he was reciting a lesson. "And it is a pleasure which we hope will be repeated in the future. None the less, this evening there is a matter of some importance to us which we would like to discuss with you."

Charles waited.

"This evening, in the bar, there was an incident which has put us away considerably," Emil went on.

"Put us *out,* darling. Not *away,*" little Frau Emil corrected gently.

"I am sorry. Put us *out,*" Emil corrected himself. "I am referring, of course, to your dispute with Mr. Gisborne."

"Dispute?" Charles repeated coolly. "I had no disput with Mr. Gisborne, Herr Emil."

"Perhaps I use the wrong word," Emil apologised. "Thanks to my wife, my English is improving, I think, but even so—would it be more accurate to say that you had a conversation with Mr. Gisborne?"

"A brief one," Charles conceded.

"About—?"

"But since you yourself were behind the bar at that time, you must have heard what we said, Herr Emil."

"That is so," Emil admitted. "He suggested that you should play bridge and you refused."

"Exactly!" Charles agreed blandly.

"But it would seem that you worded your refusal in terms which caused Mr. Gisborne displeasure," Emil ploughed on.

"Did I?" Charles asked unhelpfully.

Emil glanced appealingly at his wife, who responded at once to his appeal.

"Mr. Ravenscroft, Emil is right in saying that his English has improved considerably, but not unnaturally, he is not always able to appreciate the possible significance of a colloquialism."

"If I could speak another language than my own half as well as your husband can, Frau Emil, I would be extremely proud of myself!"

"Yes, he is good, isn't he?" she said, evidently pleased by the compliment. None the less, she was not to be diverted. "But you see, though Emil didn't realise that something you said could have more than one meaning, I did as soon as he told me about it. And we both feel that one meaning could be—important." She paused. "May I explain very frankly, Mr. Ravenscroft?"

"By all means," Charles said politely.

"Thank you. Well, it's impossible for us not to know that Mr. Gisborne is very lucky at cards. Do you agree?"

"Not entirely," Charles said with deliberate brevity, and saw that the Bergers again exchanged one of those quick glances.

"You mean—his success is due to something more than luck?" Frau Emil asked carefully.

"Undoubtedly," Charles confirmed. "He wins because he is a superlatively good player. In fact, I've never come across a better."

"Ah!" Frau Emil expelled her breath in a relieved sigh. "Then your remark to the effect that if you did play, you would *spoil Mr. Gisborne's game*, had no other significance than that you knew your game would not be up to his standard?"

"Other significance?" Charles repeated with a puzzled look. "Oh, I see! You are asking me if I intended to convey the impression that I didn't think Gisborne's game was straight and that if I had proof of that, by playing with him, I wouldn't keep my mouth shut. I can assure you that though I've often watched him play, I've never seen anything to suggest that there's anything questionable about it. Simply, he is a better exponent of the game than practically all the people with whom he plays."

There was a little silence.

"That is good," Emil said a trifle ponderously. "It is a great relief. We must apologise for having troubled you in this matter. But you will understand, of course, that the good name of an hotel is a very precious thing. We could not possibly allow—" he stopped short as if he felt that he had been on the verge of an indiscretion and Charles decided that it was time to end the interview.

"I quite understand," he said, standing up. "And I'm glad that I've been able to set your minds at rest. And now, you're very busy people, I know. I mustn't take any more of your time. Thank you for the coffee and brandy. They were first class."

And he made his escape—at least, from the Bergers. But as he was returning to the residential part of the hotel, a slight figure detached itself from a shadowy corner and stood squarely in his path.

"I want to have a word with you, Mr. Charles Ravenscroft," said Dinah ominously.

CHAPTER TWO

CHARLES'S first reaction was to take the girl firmly by the shoulders and move her bodily out of his way. But second thoughts quickly prevailed. He was reasonably sure that the Bergers had been concerned, possibly for some time, and certainly before his own advent, on the subject of Nicky Gisborne. There might even have been complaints, though if there had been, they could not have been very serious or something would have been done before this. The Bergers' anxiety for the good name of their hotel had made that clear. But Nicky had been allowed to go his own sweet way, which presumably meant that their minds had been set at rest. Now they were anxious again. The possibility that he, Charles, *had* meant to convey a warning to Nicky might mean that they thought he might make still further trouble. That was why they had given him an opportunity of making any accusations to them in private. Their relief when he had not taken advantage of that opportunity but had, in fact, given Nicky a clean bill had been obvious, and, Charles thought, had a two-fold cause.

They were reassured about Nicky. They were also sure that Charles presented no further problem since it would be impossible for him to back down after having made such a definite statement. But however convinced they might be that there would be nothing to worry about, they wouldn't take any chances. Charles was quite sure that they would keep a wary eye on him as well as on Nicky. Well, Nicky must look after himself. But as far as he was concerned, Charles was determined that nothing should happen which would suggest that he was a confirmed troublemaker. Just let that happen and he knew what the result would be. He would be asked to leave.

So it was out of the question for him to lay a finger

25

on the girl despite the fact that it was she who was making a nuisance of herself. He restrained his first impulse, but he stood his ground.

"Certainly, Miss Sherwood," he said politely. "Here? Or would you prefer somewhere a little more private?"

His easy acquiescence disconcerted Dinah. She had expected to meet with resistance and had keyed herself up for a battle of wills without giving any thought to the possibility of being overheard. Now she had been forced to realise resentfully that she didn't want a possible audience.

"You'd better come to my room," she said curtly.

Charles shook his head.

"That would hardly do, Miss Sherwood," he said gravely. "It could, you see, be open to misinterpretation," and had the satisfaction of seeing the colour surge to Dinah's cheeks. "Nor, for the same reason, can I ask you to come to mine. As an alternative, I suggest that we should go to the restaurant. Dinner must be over by now, so it would be unlikely that we would be disturbed."

"Very well," Dinah agreed, and led the way downstairs.

Charles had been right. The lights in the restaurant had been dimmed and except for a few waiters who were resetting the tables for breakfast, it was deserted. Dinah sat down at one of the tables and as Charles followed suit, found herself face to face with a man to whose appearance she had previously given little thought. She had realised, of course, that he was tall and dark, but that was all. What she had said to Nicky was true. She had no eyes for any man but him.

But now, uneasily, she couldn't miss the fact that the man had an extremely aggressive chin and a mouth that was set like a spring trap. There was something else as well though it was less easily defined. Yet Dinah knew instinctively that here was a man who was accustomed to having his own way and would not allow himself to be either persuaded or coerced into changing his mind once he had made it up.

"Yes, Miss Sherwood?" Charles asked suavely.

He was so sure of himself! So blatantly sure—probably he was the sort of man who thought all women were inferior creatures! Well, she would show him!

"Why did you go to the Bergers' flat?" she asked bluntly.

"Because they asked me to," Charles replied promptly.

"I don't believe it," Dinah contradicted flatly. "I'm quite certain that you asked to go there!"

Charles shrugged his shoulders.

"I see no way of convincing you that I'm telling the truth except to suggest that you should ask the Bergers themselves. In any case, why should I do such a thing?"

"Because you wanted to tell them lies about Nicky," Dinah retorted fiercely. "And you didn't want him to have a chance of defending himself!"

Charles regarded her thoughtfully. Red hair—and very much in love. He supposed one had to make allowances for both facts.

"That's not true," he said with a mildness which surprised Dinah—and himself.

She tossed her head. She had no *proof* of course, but none the less, she was absolutely *certain*—

"Can you deny that you and the Bergers discussed Nicky?" she demanded belligerently.

"I have no intention whatever of either denying or confirming that," Charles told her coolly.

"That means you did!" Dinah triumphed. "Because if you didn't, you'd be quick enough to say so!"

"And you'd be equally quick to tell me that you didn't believe me," Charles countered. "Isn't that so?"

"I intend to get the truth out of you," Dinah retorted stubbornly.

"And I don't intend that you should do anything of the sort," Charles told her with equal obstinacy. "I refuse categorically to repeat a private conversation simply because a near-stranger tries to bully me into doing so. Do I make myself clear, or shall I elaborate? Yes—" as he surveyed Dinah's resentful face, "I think I'd better! In my opinion, because you're a woman and I'm a man, you are presuming that good manners and sheer cowardice compel me to bow to your demands.

You couldn't be more wrong, not only because you have behaved in such an objectionable way that you have put all my masculine hackles up, but also because you have no right whatever to be given the information you're trying to extract from me."

"I've every right!" Dinah flared.

Charles's eyes narrowed speculatively.

"You mean that Gisborne put you up to tackling me? He thought you'd make a better job of it than he would?"

"I don't mean anything of the sort," Dinah denied hotly. "He's no idea—" her voice trailed away uncertainly. Not only had she not told Nicky of her determination to put this Ravenscroft man in his place once and for all, but now that, somehow or other, the interview hadn't gone in the least as she had expected it would, she certainly didn't want him to know anything about it.

"No? Well, if you'll take my advice, which of course you won't, you won't say anything about it to him. He won't like it, you know."

"I don't know what you're talking about," Dinah denied all the more emphatically because she had already come to the same conclusion herself.

Charles sighed.

"It seems to me that the scope of your education hasn't been as extensive as it should have been! Hasn't your father ever told you—"

"My father is dead," Dinah interrupted curtly.

"I'm sorry. Brothers, then? Boy cousins?"

"I've no family at all," Dinah explained, unconscious of the wistful little droop of her mouth.

"Ah, that explains it! Well, my child, for the sake of my own sex as well as for your good, I'll elucidate. Now listen, because it's important! No man worth his salt likes to have a woman take up cudgels on his behalf. Oh, he likes to know he's got her backing, of course. What he doesn't like is for her to behave in such a way that people get the impression that he's not capable of standing on his own feet or that he's hiding behind her petticoats. He feels it makes him look a fool.

Masculine vanity, if you like, but none the less, it's one of the facts of life that you can't afford to ignore. And now—" he stood up, "I don't think we have anything more to say to one another, have we?"

Dinah bit her lip. She had been stupid to pit her small strength against this man's terrific ego. She simply hadn't had a chance of success.

But while it was bad enough to have to admit that, there was something that was still worse. She had made a complete mess of it, and the last thing she wanted was for Nicky to know that. Well, Charles was the only other person who knew of her indiscretion and since he had advised her not to tell Nicky of their encounter presumably he, too, intended to keep his own counsel. But that put her under an obligation to him, which was humiliating to the last degree. It also meant that she must never again cross swords with him lest, in retaliation, he should break his implied commitment to hold his tongue.

Slowly Dinah stood up and for a brief moment their eyes met. Hers widened incredulously. With a choking catch of her breath she pushed past Charles and fled out of the restaurant.

For in those dark, penetrating eyes she hadn't seen triumph or contempt or amusement, none of which would have surprised her.

Pity. Unmistakable pity. That was what he had felt for her, and he hadn't tried to disguise it.

It was the last straw.

Dinah went to bed that night convinced that she wouldn't sleep a wink. But it had been a strenuous day, much of which she had spent out of doors. She was fast asleep almost as soon as her head touched the pillow. Nor did she wake up until Anna brought in her morning tea and drew the curtains to let the sunshine come pouring in.

"Is a lofely day," she announced with a pride which suggested that she was personally responsible for its beauty. "The *fräulein* skis today?"

"Yes," Dinah said joyfully. "I have a lesson this morning."

"Ah, with handsome young instructor!" Anna said archly. "A heartbreaker, that one, *nicht wahr*?"

Dinah smiled, but when Anna had gone, the smile faded. She set down her tea and sat hugging her knees, wishing that Anna hadn't said that. It suggested that Nicky was fickle—that he had had a lot of affairs. Of course, she knew it wasn't true, but all the same—

Then her thoughts turned to last night's events and her heart really sank. Just what sort of a pickle had she got herself into? She was completely at Charles's mercy, and if he chose to be vindictive—

Then suddenly she gave a little crow of triumph. How silly she had been! At least, she had if he had told the truth about it being the Bergers who had sought that interview. And it could be, because, after all, Emil had heard how deliberately offensive Charles had been to Nicky, and judging by his expression, hadn't liked it. So had he and his wife taken Charles to task for making himself unpleasant? Oh, very tactfully and discreetly, of course, but it was something that had happened once before, Nicky had told her. There had been some unpleasantness and the man concerned, just like Charles, had been invited to have coffee with the Bergers. The next day he had left the hotel, though there was still another week of his holiday to run.

Yes, it could be that way, and it certainly explained why Charles had been so reluctant to tell her just what had passed between himself and the Bergers. Why, *he* might be leaving today, just as the other man had!

But even if he didn't go, she could be quite sure that he wouldn't speak of her indiscretion, because the last thing he could want would be for the matter to be resurrected in any shape or form. So what was there for her to worry about?

She finished her tea, scrambled out of bed and bathed and dressed in record time, with the result that she was down to breakfast before Nicky put in an appearance. Charles was already at his table, but he was immersed in his newspaper and didn't notice her pass him— which was rather a pity. It ruined her plan to smile at him just as if nothing had happened—which would have got him guessing. However, one can't have every-thing, she decided philosophically, and anyway, Nicky joined her at that moment and she forgot all about Charles.

After breakfast the two of them tramped together to the ski club and not only was the sun shining, but Nicky was in the highest of spirits. Nothing was left of last night's anger—and he *had* been angry to the point of leaving the hotel and not returning for dinner. As a result, Dinah had been scared and near to despair. Now he was all smiles and gaiety and Dinah fell happily under the spell of his charm.

And the final touch to her happiness was added when Nicky announced that he was promoting her.

"No more nursery slopes for you, my sweet," he told her gaily. "You're ready now for something a bit more exciting—and demanding."

Mentally Dinah crossed her fingers, but though she was nervous lest she wasn't able to live up to Nicky's opinion of her ability, it never occurred to her to question his decision. Not, for one moment, did she imagine that, because of their special relationship, he would treat her more indulgently than any other of his pupils. Nicky, off duty, was lighthearted and charming, but on his job he was a martinet, allowing no slack-ness and no excuses, even from her. In which, of course, Dinah knew that he was quite right. He was the expert and he knew his job. In fact, he was so good at it that Dinah sometimes wondered why he was content to stay at a little place like Alpenglühen when, at a more fashionable centre, he would have so much more scope. And when she remarked on this, he admitted that she was right.

"More cash—yes. But there are other considerations. For instance, the more fashionable the resort, the more expensive the hotels—or any other accommodation, in fact. I doubt if I'd earn sufficient extra to bridge the gap and—" he grimaced in a ruefully boyish way that made Dinah's heart turn over, "I must admit that I do like my creature comforts! Not a very noble sentiment, I'm afraid, but at least I'm being honest!"

31

So Dinah dropped the subject, though her belief in his pre-eminence never wavered. Nicky, she was convinced, could command any reward he chose, because it wasn't only that his own skill was so good. He had a gift for teaching which made even his least promising pupils gain some confidence and expertise.

Certainly that morning he inspired Dinah to a performance of which she hadn't thought herself capable, and it was sheer bliss to receive Nicky's praise which was never given lightly.

"A little longer and you'll not need me to coach you any more," he told her as they went back to the club house.

"If you say things like that, then next time I'm out, I won't be so good," she told him saucily. "*I'll* see to that!"

"Now, look here, young woman—" Nicky began with mock severity, but at that moment he was hailed by the club secretary.

"Hi, Gisborne, a telephone message for you! Mrs. Fairbrother rang to say she can't make it this morning. Some mix-up over friends arriving a day before they were expected. Damn careless woman!"

"Oh well, there it is," Nicky shrugged easily, glancing at his watch. "Anyone else to take Mrs. Fairbrother's place? No? Then that gives me a clear hour of freedom! Dinah, how would you like it if we indulged ourselves at the Schokoladehaus?"

"Marvellous!" Dinah exclaimed fervently.

Usually, after her session with Nicky, time hung heavily on her hands since this was the height of the season and he was in great demand. She was on quite friendly terms with some of the other club members, but she had never been really absorbed into any of the little groups because she had never responded to any overtures of friendship which had been made. If she couldn't be with Nicky, she really preferred her own company, for then she could at least think about him. But now, at the prospect of this unexpected treat, she glowed and sparkled with happiness.

The Schokoladehaus, the most popular place of its

kind in Alpenglühen, was doing brisk business when they arrived, but they were lucky enough to find a table and sat down opposite one another. Nicky smiled as he looked into Dinah's eloquent face. No one, seeing it, could doubt that she was happy and that she was head over heels in love—with him. It gave him a sense of confidence that he didn't always have and mixed with other feelings was one of downright gratitude. She certainly did something for a chap's ego!

They were served with brimming cups of chocolate topped with a small mountain of whipped cream and for a further indulgence, tucked into the fantastic cream pastries for which the Haus was famous.

"This is bliss!" Dinah remarked between mouthfuls. "I know perfectly well that I shall put on weight at such an alarming rate that none of my clothes will fit me, but at the moment I can't seem to worry about it."

"I should think not," Nicky said with a touch of asperity which surprised Dinah. "Heavens above, one must, now and again, leave consequences to take care of themselves or life isn't worth living. Hallo!" his voice changed. "See who's just sat down over there."

Dinah looked in the direction which he indicated and saw that the newcomer was Charles. She shrugged her shoulders.

"I feel in such a beneficient frame of mind that I'm even prepared to admit that he's as much right to come here as we have—though I rather wish he hadn't. Oh, my *goodness*!"

She jumped to her feet so hastily that her chair went spinning and to Nicky's startled gaze she seemed almost to fly across the room in the direction of the door by which they had entered it. He turned sharply and was in time to see Dinah make a grab at the arm of an elderly, white-haired lady who was swaying on her feet as if on the point of fainting. And even as he watched, the two women were joined by a man who, with what Nicky felt was nauseating self-assurance, at once took charge. Charles Ravenscroft, of course! It would be!

"All right, I've got her," Charles said quietly to

Dinah. "Turn that chair round, will you, Miss Sherwood? That's better!" as he eased the limp figure into the chair though he still kept a sustaining arm round the slender shoulders. "Now, don't try to talk," he said authoritatively to the ailing woman. "Just relax —that's the way!" Automatically the fingers of his free hand sought the pulse in the slender wrist, and though he made no comment, Dinah saw that the muscles of his mouth tightened. "One of you girls—" he looked round the little group of startled waitresses who, wide-eyed, were clustering round. "Go and get a glass of water—hurry!"

When the water arrived, he told Dinah to hold the glass to the lips of his patient—it was impossible, he found, not to think of her as that—

"Carefully," he warned, "so that she can just sip it,"

Oddly, Dinah felt no resentment at the way in which he was giving orders. In fact, if she thought about it at all, it was with thankfulness that there was somebody who knew what to do.

For a moment or so the white-haired woman sipped thirstily. Then she whispered: "Enough!" and made an effort to sit more erect.

"No, keep still a little longer," Charles said firmly, and to his amazement, his patient lifted his head and he saw that in her deep brown eyes there was a twinkle of genuine amusement. He pulled himself together sharply. Evidently she had guessed what his profession was, although why she should find that amusing he didn't see. Still, he must be careful.

"Does anyone know who—" he began, but at that moment the proprietress of the Schokoladhaus bustled in. News of the emergency must have been relayed to her, but that was all, for when she saw the still figure, she gave vent to an exclamation of horror.

"It is the Contessa—the Contessa Farini! But I do not understand! Where is Greta—her maid? The Contessa *never* leaves her home without Greta. Always she is there."

"Greta—coming," the Contessa explained briefly, and at that moment Greta arrived.

34

She was a tall, spare woman who gave the impression of tremendous, concentrated energy. She took the situation in at a glance and immediately dipped into her capacious handbag, producing a little capsule. She broke it into the clean handkerchief which Charles had instantly produced from his pocket and held it so that the Contessa could inhale the vapour. To Dinah's intense relief, a little colour returned to the white cheeks.

"Better," she whispered, and would have tried to stand up had Charles not laid a retaining hand on her shoulder.

"Not for a little while yet," he advised, and then, turning to Greta: "How did your mistress get here? Did she walk?"

"Nein, nein!" Greta sounded positively shocked at the idea. "In her car she came, of course. It will arrive shortly. Fritz has his orders."

Relieved, Charles turned to Dinah and saw that Nicky had joined them and was speaking to her.

"I'll simply have to go, Dinah," he said apologetically. "I can't risk a black mark for being late."

"No, of course not," Dinah agreed, guiltily aware that in the excitement she had forgotten all about Nicky. She conjured up a smile for him. "Thank you for my treat, Nicky!"

"Rather ruined, actually," he commented resentfully without troubling to lower his voice. "Oh, nobody's fault, of course," he added quickly, seeing her troubled look. "Just my luck! Be seeing you!"

"Yes," Dinah agreed, and her eyes followed him wistfully as he vanished through the doorway.

A little later a message was brought to say that the car had arrived. With Charles's help, the Contessa stood up and instantly turned to Dinah.

"Thank you, my dear, for your great kindness to—a stranger," she said softly, and momentarily laid her hand on Dinah's. Then she turned to Charles. "And you, too, Mr. Ravenscroft! I am deeply in your debt. And I would be still more deeply in it. Will you give me your arm out to my car?"

"With your permission, Contessa, I will do more than

35

that," Charles said with a courtliness which surprised Dinah. "May I have the honour of carrying you out to your car?"

The Contessa giggled—there was really no other description for the youthful sound that passed her lips.

"You don't think that such a thing might be open to misinterpretation?" she asked mischievously.

Charles laughed responsively. From some women of her age such a suggestion would have been both absurd and distasteful, but from the Contessa, it was both charming and amusing.

"I wish I could think so, Contessa!" Charles said gallantly. "Now, if you'll put your arms round my neck—splendid!"

He lifted her effortlessly and for the first time Dinah realised what a splendid physique he had. Admittedly, the Contessa was very slightly built, but to be able to swing her up as if she was a child—that was quite something! Then she noticed that the Contessa's handbag lay forgotten on the floor and picking it up, she followed Charles and his burden out to the waiting car.

The Contessa was tucked carefully into the back of it, but even then Charles lingered, leaning in to say something very earnestly, though Dinah could not hear what it was. But she saw that the Contessa nodded and her lips clearly shaped the words: "I promise!"

Charles stood erect, the bag was handed in and the car started slowly up the steep gradient of the hill.

Side by side, Dinah and Charles watched it out of sight. Dinah drew a deep breath.

"What a—what a *person*!" she said with awed admiration.

"Yes, indeed!" Charles concurred fervently. "I've never met anyone like her before."

"Nor have I!" Dinah declared, but she looked slightly perplexed. "And yet, you know, I had the most peculiar feeling that I'd seen her before—though certainly not since I've been in Alpenglühen."

"That's odd," Charles looked at her thoughtfully. "I had just the same impression, although, like you, th¦

is the first time I've seen her here. There was something about her eyes—"

Dinah shook her head.

"It wasn't her eyes as far as I was concerned," she told him. "It was her voice that sounded familiar." She pondered and then shook her head. "No, it's no use. I can't remember. Still, I'm glad I've met her now. It was quite an experience."

"It certainly was," Charles agreed, and then, without consulting one another, they fell into step and walked back to the hotel together.

Neither had much to say. Dinah was still puzzling over her conviction that, absurd though the idea was, this wasn't her first meeting with the Contessa.

Charles had two quite different problems to perplex him.

That heart attack had, he was reasonably sure, been brought on by a sudden shock. And since, when the Contessa had come in, he had noticed that her eyes were riveted on Dinah's face, then wasn't it reasonable to assume that *she* had been the cause of the shock? Yet how could that make sense, since Dinah was entirely oblivious to the possibility of such a thing?

The other problem that vexed him was of less importance though still puzzling.

How the devil had it come about that the Contessa had known his name?

To the amazement of both Dinah and Charles, news of what had happened at the Schokoladehaus had preceded them to the hotel. In fact, they had no sooner entered it than this became evident. Dr. Plumber, dressed in an immaculate city suit, was in the foyer and he immediately accosted Charles.

"Ah, Ravenscroft!" he began importantly. "I'm glad you've come. I'm just off to the Chalet Farini and I shall be glad if you will describe the Contessa's symptoms to me as accurately as possible."

His manner suggested that actually he hadn't much hope of accuracy from a layman, and though Charles knew that he was partly to blame since he had taken such care not to let his profession be known, he none the less felt his hackles rising. He was all the less willing to go out of his way to be helpful because little Frau Emil was hovering in the background and her anxious face told Charles that far from having been asked to go to the Chalet, Dr. Plumber was making the most of the opportunity to insinuate himself there unasked.

"There's little to tell," Charles replied coolly. "The Contessa was entering the restaurant when she began to sway to an extent which suggested she might fall. Both Miss Sherwood and I happened to notice and we were in time to support her. Between us, we got the lady into a chair, and really, that's all."

"But I understood she was given treatment by you," Dr. Plumber said accusingly.

"Other than having water brought for her to drink, no," Charles denied shortly.

"But she was given something to inhale, surely? That is what I was told," Dr. Plumber protested.

"Oh, that!" Charles shook his head. "No, that wasn't my doing. The Contessa's maid arrived almost immediately and she had a phial of—" he checked himself on the brink of giving the correct name to the preparation and substituted : "something or other which she broke into a handkerchief and held for the Contessa to inhale."

"I see, I see." Dr. Plumber assumed his mantle of self-importance again. "Well, thank you, Ravenscroft. That is some help. But I mustn't delay further—"

"As a matter of fact, I did suggest to the Contessa that it would be a good idea if she got in touch with her doctor at once. And she promised she would," Charles said hopefully.

But he might as well have tried to halt an avalanche once it was in motion. Murmuring something about two heads being better than one, Dr. Plumber bustled off, leaving three thoroughly disgruntled people gazing after him. Frau Emil was the first to speak.

"Silly, bumptious old know-all," she exclaimed fervently. "Poking his nose in where he's not wanted! Oh well, I'd better phone through to the Chalet and

38

warn them that he's coming. With any luck, Dr. Schwartz will at least be on his way and he'll see to it that the Contessa isn't bothered by that—that—" she left the sentence trailing as she hurried into the office and through the glass partition, they could see her talking earnestly on the telephone. A moment or so later she rejoined them.

"That's all right!" she told them with considerable satisfaction. "Actually, Dr. Schwartz had just arrived, so I was able to explain to him. He said: '*Over my dead body*!' so that's put a spoke into that tuft-hunter's wheel! Which is just as well, because otherwise we'd have been hearing everlastingly about '*My patient the Contessa*!' Ugh! Oh dear!" Her voice altered suddenly as Emil came down the stairs and she grimaced with comical ruefulness. "I ought not to say things like that. It's one of the first rules for being an hotelier that one mustn't criticise one's guests—particularly to other guests!"

"Don't worry, Frau Emil," Charles said reassuringly. "Wild horses wouldn't drag it out of us, would they, Miss Sherwood?"

"Of course not," Dinah confirmed vigorously. "And it was simply marvellous to hear you say just the things I've wanted to say ever since he came here—only I was afraid it was just being nasty!"

"That goes for me, too!" Charles admitted, and with a flashing smile distributed evenly between them, Frau Emil ran off to join her husband.

For a moment or two neither Charles nor Dinah spoke. Then Dinah sighed and said regretfully:

"I do wish that hadn't happened."

"What—the little Frau's indiscretion? It'll do no harm. We won't tell tales out of school and it must have relieved her feelings considerably."

"I expect so," Dinah agreed. "But I didn't mean that. I meant Dr. Plumber going up to the Chalet. You see, I'd been thinking I'd like to go up there myself tomorrow. Oh, not expecting to see the Contessa, but just to enquire. But now—" she shook her head.

"Following Plumber's intrusion, you don't feel that

you can," Charles finished for her. "I know. I'd had the same idea, but I agree with you, it's out of the question now. Of course, one could phone—"

"Ye-es," Dinah demurred. "But somehow that's awfully impersonal because it's so easy. And—and I did like her so."

Charles looked at her thoughtfully. Clearly there was more to this young redhead than he had at first appreciated.

"Or, of course, one could send flowers," he suggested, and Dinah's face cleared as if by magic.

"Of *course*!" She beamed at him. "That would be perfect, particularly as one could write a little message to go with them. I *am* glad you thought of that, Mr. Ravenscroft!"

"Without wishing to appear to blow my own trumpet, so am I," Charles confessed. "It solves my problem as well as yours. I wonder—" he hesitated. "Would you mind if I come to the florists with you, Miss Sherwood? Just to make sure that our selection of flowers differ from one another," he added quickly as he saw the surprise in Dinah's eyes.

"Oh—why, yes, of course," she agreed. "I thought I'd go this afternoon so that they can be delivered first thing tomorrow."

"Excellent!" Charles replied. "About—three o'clock?"

Dinah agreed and went up to her room while Charles, in a reflective mood, went into the deserted bar.

It had suddenly occurred to him that the hospital and his work—even his recent success—seemed to be very far away. *Here* and *now* seemed so much more important, and that he found disconcerting. Always before he had contrived to avoid personal involvement in other people's affairs. Now, through no volition on his part, that was certainly not the case.

For a moment he felt an acute stab of apprehension as if one of the mainstays of his own personality had suddenly proved to be faulty. Then he shrugged the notion away.

After all, what need was there to worry? On holiday, everyone behaved differently from what they normally

40

did—with the possible exception of Dr. Plumber. Once he got back to work, he would assume his real personality, Charles told himself firmly. And this interlude would fade into the past and be forgotten.

Nicky was too busy that day to come back to the hotel for lunch, so Dinah didn't see him until shortly before dinner time, and by then he appeared to have lost all interest in the Contessa or even to have forgotten all about the incident until Dinah referred to it.

"The *Contessa*!" he exclaimed with a decided show of excitement. "I didn't realise—are you sure, Dinah?"

"Oh yes," Dinah replied, trying not to acknowledge a little sense of chill at his reaction to the news. "But it doesn't really matter who she is, does it? I mean, the important thing was that she needed help, and I'm glad I was able to give it to her."

"Yes, of course, darling," Nicky said quickly, and smiled at her in that very special way of his that tore at Dinah's heart strings. "And you mustn't think I'm a title snob—as I think you did, didn't you?"

"Well—" Dinah said hesitantly.

"Well, it sounded like it!" Nicky filled in for her. "No, it wasn't that! It's simply that it seems to me there's a sort of *mystique* about the Contessa." He frowned as if he was trying to marshal his thoughts. "It's a bit difficult to explain just what I mean, but if ever her name is mentioned, I always get the impression that, locally, she's regarded as someone who is—who is made of finer clay than the rest of us. Not a deity, but all the same—somehow set apart. I expect that sounds absurd—" he looked enquiringly at Dinah.

"Not to me," she averred. "Even in the little time I was with her I felt that she's a very special person."

"Yes, that's it," Nicky sounded relieved at her understanding. "A very special person. And as a result, I must admit to having been very anxious to see her. But that's all. Am I forgiven?"

"There's nothing to forgive," Dinah told him happily. And then, as an afterthought: "I've arranged to have some flowers sent to her tomorrow."

41

"Have you?" Nicky smiled at her again. "How like you, sweetheart! I'm sure, however special she may be, she'll appreciate your thought for her."

Dinah smiled responsively, but she felt guilty. She didn't want to have any secrets from Nicky, but somehow circumstances seemed to force her to. She couldn't, of course, tell him about Dr. Plumber, because she'd promised not to, and anyway, that wasn't of any real importance to either of them. What troubled her was that she had felt it was quite impossible to tell him that Charles, too, was sending flowers, and even more difficult to admit that they had visited the florists together.

Surely Nicky would have understood that it was just something which had happened quite naturally and that, pleasant though Charles had made himself, it hadn't been of the least importance to her.

But the worst of it was that, by not telling him, she had put herself into a false position. Now, if he were to hear of it from someone else, it would be understandable if he assumed that it had been something which she wanted to keep from him.

"The trouble is, I'm not used to being deceitful," poor Dinah thought ruefully. "I'm glad I'm not, of course, but it does make life difficult sometimes."

"A penny for them!" Nicky said suddenly.

"Oh, they're not worth that," Dinah disclaimed quickly.

"No? But you were looking as if all the cares of the world had suddenly descended on your shoulders—and I don't like to see you troubled, Dinah. What's wrong, darling?"

"Oh—" Dinah said breathlessly, and grasped at the first excuse which offered itself. "It's just that I've had a letter from the solicitor who—who looks after things for me and he sent *masses* of documents for me to read and sign. And the bother is, when I have read them, I still don't understand what they mean. And it worries me."

" 'Fraid I can't be of any help to you there," Nicky confessed ruefully. "I'm a complete duffer where legal matters are concerned. When they do crop up, I just cross my fingers and sign! So far, that seems to have worked quite well."

"Yes, but—" Dinah began, and paused. Sooner or later Nicky would have to know about her money. Wouldn't this be a good opportunity for telling him, without putting it into so many words, that though she wasn't wealthy by many standards, she was certainly better off than he was? "I think," she said slowly, "that all men understand these things better than women do—certainly better than I do! Nicky, would it be too much of a bother for you to go through the wretched things for me?"

"My dear!" Nicky said deprecatingly. "What's the point of me doing that? Honestly, it's not my line!"

"All the same—will you?" Dinah persisted.

"What's the good?" Nicky asked, shaking his head, and then seeing the disappointment in her eyes: "Well, all right. But only if you'll promise not to put too much dependence on anything I say—though, of course, I'll do my best."

He kept his word. Late into the night he pored over the documents and the covering letter which had accompanied them, and referred frequently to the financial pages of an English newspaper which he had found discarded in the writing-room waste-paper basket.

At last he was satisfied that he could conscientiously tell Dinah to go ahead and sign the documents, most of which referred to the purchase or sale of various stocks and shares.

But he had learned more than that from his efforts. He knew now that Dinah had not inherited a comparatively small legacy from her father which she was squandering recklessly on this holiday, as he had thought might be the case. On the contrary, assuming, as he thought was reasonable, that these transactions referred to only part of her inheritance, she not only had a very pleasant income but also, of course, a quite considerable amount of capital.

He folded the papers and put them back into their envelope, but, late though it was, he sat on for a long time at the little table, deep in thought. He was a poor man with little or no prospects. By comparison, Dinah was rich. It was an awkward and delicate situation and one, he knew, which would require careful handling. That Dinah trusted him completely he had no doubt, but nor had he any illusions as to how nine people out of ten would regard him—as a fortune-hunter who had taken advantage of an inexperienced girl who had no family to advise and protect her.

He sighed deeply. Yes, Dinah *did* trust him—but supposing, one day, she was somehow persuaded to listen to the opinion of the world? It *could* happen—and then what? Unpleasantness and disillusionment—and they were the last things Nicky wanted.

His handsome face was set in unusually grim and determined lines as he finally came to a decision.

There was only one thing for it. He would have to trust to luck—after all, by the law of averages, it was about time that it changed for the better!

None the less, he proposed to give that luck every assistance which lay in his power. So far, thank goodness, he had been absolutely straight with Dinah. Well, he would continue to be that. He would leave her in no doubt just how tricky such a state of affairs could be. He might—yes, he would—tell her that she would be wiser to send him packing. He would give her every chance—

He turned in with a mind at ease and slept peacefully for what was left of the night.

Decidedly, honesty was the best—the only—policy.

CHAPTER THREE

DINAH came down to breakfast the next morning feeling an unease which was not lessened by the fact that Nicky had not yet arrived. Almost certainly, she was sure, he had been startled, if nothing more, by the discovery that she was so much better off than he was. Dinah sighed. She loved Nicky for his pride, but it did make for problems, not the least of which was the fact that even now he didn't know the whole story. There was so much more money than that dealt with by Mr. Jenner, the solicitor. There was the rest of the capital over which she already had control and the further amount which was in trust until she was twenty-five. If Nicky found what he already knew to be unpalatable, how would he feel when he knew all the facts?

So her smile, when he did finally arrive, was tremulous and vanished altogether when she saw how glum he looked. Breakfast was a silent meal at which neither of them ate very much, and it didn't surprise Dinah when, at the end of it, Nicky said abruptly:

"Dinah, you and I have got to have a talk—now. If you'll go to the lounge, I'll join you in a few minutes."

Dinah nodded speechlessly, convinced that she had been right. And when, a little later, he rejoined her, bringing with him the big legal envelope, her worst fears were quickly confirmed.

"I've been through everything pretty carefully," he said in that same abrupt way. "And as far as I'm able to judge from studying the share prices in an English newspaper, your solicitor's suggestions seem perfectly sound. I don't think you need be afraid to sign everything."

"Oh good," Dinah said faintly, taking the envelope from him.

Nicky seemed to be on the point of saying more, but changed his mind. He turned his back on her and walked over to the window where he stood staring out, shoulders hunched, hands thrust deep into his pockets. Dinah swallowed convulsively, unable to break the frightening silence. The minutes ticked on—

Suddenly Nicky swung round.

"Dinah, why didn't you tell me?" he burst out angrily.

She didn't try to pretend that she didn't understand. It was too serious for that.

"I was afraid," she explained simply.

He gave her a quick, resentful look.

"You mean you didn't trust me," he said morosely. "You thought I was the sort of chap that would marry a girl for her money!"

"No!" Dinah contradicted passionately. "No, it wasn't that at all. It was just the other way round. I— I was afraid, if you knew, you wouldn't want to marry me." And she realised, with surprise, that this was the first time that *marriage* had been spoken of between them. They had told each other of their love and, of course, that was what really mattered. But now, despite her anxiety, Dinah felt a thrill of excitement. "You see, she went on hurriedly, "I know how proud you are, Nicky. I knew just how you'd feel about—about—"

"About living on my wife's money," Nicky said bitterly. "Well, I do feel that. It's an impossible position —if I could match what you've got or had any prospect of being able to do that in the future, then perhaps it wouldn't matter. But I've absolutely nothing except the pittance I earn and there's no chance, as far as I can see, of it ever being any different."

"You think—money is as important as all that?" Dinah asked painfully. "When people really love one another?"

A muscle twitched at the corner of Nicky's mouth.

"But that's just it," he insisted with smouldering ferocity. "What I'm afraid of is that, once the glamour had faded a bit, you'd begin to wonder—"

"Nicky, how could I when I know that you knew nothing about it until *after* you told me that you loved me?" she protested.

46

But it was of no use.

"So you didn't trust me!" he accused bitterly. "You were afraid to tell me, weren't you?"

"Yes, I've told you I was," Dinah acknowledged desperately. "Not because I thought you'd pretend to love me for the sake of my money, but because I was afraid you'd feel exactly as you do about it. Oh, Nicky, *please* try to understand! It was so difficult to know how to tell you, and then this—" she indicated the big envelope, "came and I thought—if you saw what it was all about—it would—"

"Break it to me gently?" Nicky asked grimly. "But that sounds as if you haven't told me everything even yet! Ah, I thought not!" as Dinah's eyes widened apprehensively. "So you've got quite a bit more than you were going to tell me about, haven't you?"

"Yes," Dinah admitted briefly.

"I thought so! And how," Nicky went on relentlessly, "can you be sure that I haven't known all about it right from the beginning? You can't know! Oh, not from you, of course, but how do you know that someone didn't recognise you and tell me how well heeled you are?"

Dinah's heart froze with chill certainty. She knew exactly what Nicky was going to say next. Nor was she wrong.

"You see? You can't know!" he slung at her. "If you've got any sense at all, Dinah, you'll send me packing. And if you don't, then I shall opt out, that's all!"

"And break my heart?" Dinah whispered, turning her face from him.

A sound that seemed to be partly a groan and partly an oath was wrung from Nicky's lips.

"What in heaven's name am I to do?" he exclaimed desperately. "You're so sweet, Dinah. I love you so much. But how can I prove it to you?"

Dinah's sensitive lips quivered.

"You don't have to prove it, Nicky. I *know*." She knew from the way he shook his head that she hadn't convinced him yet she was none the less encouraged to go on. "If—if it was the other way about, if it was *your*

47

money, would you think it was because of it that I want to marry you?"

"That's different," he insisted. "I mean, it's the usual way for things to be. One takes it for granted that the husband does the providing. And anyway—" his expression softened to one of tenderness, "nothing would ever convince me that you'd be a fortune-hunter, my sweet Dinah!"

"Then you ought to understand that nothing will ever convince me that you are!" Dinah retorted triumphantly. "Don't you see, Nicky, that's the whole thing. We *know* each other and we *love* one another! So there's nothing to worry about!"

"I see what you mean," Nicky admitted dubiously. "But—"

"Nicky, listen!" Dinah implored eagerly. "If you feel so strongly about it, then there is a way out. I'll give all my money away—to charities or something—"

Nicky looked at her with something like awe in his blue eyes.

"You mean you—you'd do that for my sake?" he stammered. "Do I mean as much as all that to you?"

Dinah nodded silently, but her eyes were like stars as Nicky took her hands in his.

"It would be a way out," he acknowledged slowly. "Perhaps the best way. And yet—oh, don't you see, Dinah, because you trust me so, I mustn't think only of my own feelings. I've got to think for you as well. I've got to face up to the fact that your money is all that stands between you and the poverty which is all that I can offer you. Oh, I know—" as her lips parted in protest. "You wouldn't mind giving up the luxuries you're used to in exchange for happiness. But I'm not talking about luxuries. I'm talking about the downright necessities of life. I can only just make out decently on my own, you know. For two of us it would be downright penury. Which is something I ought to have thought of long before now! I'd no right whatever to tell you that I love you—only there it is. I fell head over heels—" he smiled ruefully. "You're so sweet, Dinah! How could I help it?"

There was a brief, blissful interlude and then Dinah became severely practical.

"I could get a job," she pointed out. "Perhaps even at this hotel—"

Nicky sighed and ran his fingers distractedly through his crisp golden hair.

"I don't know, Dinah," he confessed. "I just don't know. It's all come as rather a shock to me, you know, and my first impulse—well, I've told you. But there's more to it—give me time to get used to the way things are, then perhaps I'll see clearly what's the best thing for us to do."

"Of course," Dinah said thankfully. "And—and until you say, I won't do anything."

"Bless you," Nicky said fervently.

A day or so later Dinah had a letter which bore no stamp, and when she opened it, she found that it was from the Contessa.

"Dear Dinah," it began, "I hope you don't mind me calling you that, but it is a name I have always liked and your charming gift encourages me to believe that you have friendly feelings towards me.

"I am going to presume on that belief by asking you to give some of your time to a very lonely woman. Will you have tea with me here tomorrow, Thursday, at about 4 o'clock? It would give me so much pleasure and will give me the opportunity of thanking you personally for the lovely flowers.

"Will you telephone to say whether you will be able to come or not?   Yours sincerely,
                                        Isobel Farini."

Dinah was delighted, not only that she had given the Contessa pleasure, but also that she would be seeing her again. For she *had* taken an instant liking to the elegant woman who, though she was so much older than Dinah herself was, had shown such a marvellously youthful spirit. Why, she had practically flirted with Charles Ravenscroft who, bleak individual though

49

Dinah had felt him to be, had responded with every sign of appreciation!

And thinking of Charles made her wonder if he, too, had had a letter from the Contessa, and even more important, whether it had contained a similar invitation to her own.

With that in mind, she hesitated momentarily before telephoning the Chalet. Nicky might not feel too happy about it if she and Charles did, apparently, go together. But not only was it quite impossible to question either Charles or the Contessa on that point, but Dinah wanted most desperately to accept the invitation. The feeling that she had met the Contessa before was as elusive but none the less just as persistent as ever. Perhaps, if she were to hear the Contessa talking again, she would remember.

So she rang through to the Chalet, but Greta, who answered her call, interrupted her before she had completed her message.

"One moment, please, *Fräulein*," she said briskly. "The Contessa has given me instructions—she wishes to speak to you herself. Please to wait."

Dinah did as she was asked. There was a confused sound of voices in the background and then the Contessa came on the line.

"Dinah?" The voice had just the same warm quality about it which Dinah remembered, but surely there was rather a worrying hint of breathlessness about it?

"Yes, Dinah speaking," she confirmed. "I should love to accept your invitation, Contessa—if you're quite sure I shan't tire you?"

The Contessa laughed softly.

"No, my dear, I assure you that will not happen! On the contrary, I am quite sure that your visit will do me good. It will give me something to think of other than my own silly aches and pains—and that in itself would be a relief quite apart from the pleasure it will give me to see you again. So—four o'clock tomorrow?"

"Four o'clock," Dinah confirmed, but after she had rung off, she stood staring at the telephone in a perplexed way. Was it her imagination or had the Contessa murmured something else just as she was about to hang up? Something that sounded like a very soft, very reverent : "*Thank God*!"?

But of course, that was unlikely. Dinah didn't doubt but that the Contessa was pleased that she was going to visit her, but surely it was too trifling a matter to warrant such emphatic gratitude? Yes, she must have misheard.

By chance, Charles was in the foyer as she passed through it and she seized the opportunity to find out, if possible, if he, too, had been invited to the Chalet. "Oh—Mr. Ravenscroft, I've had such a charming letter from the Contessa—" she began.

"So have I," Charles said with a smile. "It would seem that we hit the nail right on the head!"

"You did, you mean," Dinah said honestly. "It was your idea, remember!"

"So it was," Charles agreed. "And one I'm still quite proud of, though I don't think it was really surprising that I had it. There's something about the Contessa—" he frowned as if unable to explain just what he had in mind, but Dinah had no such difficulty.

"She's the sort of person that *should* have flowers sent to her," she finished for him. "It just seems natural, somehow."

"Yes, that's it," Charles acknowledged. "And yet I've the impression that her life hasn't been a matter of flowers, flowers all the way."

"Perhaps that's why we both wanted to give her some," Dinah suggested soberly.

"Could be." Charles lifted his hand in salute and went on his way.

"Well, that's not got me any forrarder," Dinah thought ruefully. "Queer that he didn't tell me if she'd invited him—but then I didn't tell him either, so perhaps he said nothing in case I hadn't been! Oh dear, it could be a little bit difficult if, after all, we do meet there!"

But when she arrived at the Chalet the following afternoon, there was no sign of Charles, and judging by the fact that there were only two cups and saucers on

51

the attractively laid tea-tray, he wasn't expected. Dinah felt relieved.

The Contessa was lying on a sofa and she made no attempt to get up when Dinah was shown into the room, but she held out both hands and there was no mistaking the sincerity of her welcome.

"Dear child!" Her voice was warm and caressing. "You are so welcome! It is rarely that I have *young* visitors so you are like a breath of spring to me! Sit down where I can feast my eyes on your pretty face!"

As Dinah did so, she felt that the nervous tension which the prospect of this visit had caused had now completely vanished, and that for an unexpected reason. Despite the warmth of the Contessa's greeting, Dinah had a conviction that *she* was nervous, though it didn't seem to make sense. But sense or not, Dinah was conscious of an overwhelming rush of protectiveness towards the older woman and it gave an added confidence to her reply.

"I'm glad you feel like that, Contessa, for I did so want to see you again. In fact, I would have called to enquire how you were, only—only—"

"Only you felt that Dr. Plumber's intrusion made that impossible," the Contessa suggested understandingly with a little grimace of distaste.

"Well, yes. And Mr. Ravenscroft felt the same way," Dinah replied earnestly, all the more anxious to give Charles his due because—well, perhaps because he hadn't had an invitation to tea.

"Yes, I formed the opinion that he is a sensitive man." And while Dinah was recovering from her surprise at the remark, the Contessa went on thoughtfully: "And a very reliable one, don't you agree?"

"Yes," Dinah found herself saying unhesitatingly. "One couldn't imagine circumstances in which he'd lose his head."

"Exactly," the Contessa agreed. "But being a very curious and inquisitive old lady with far too much time on her hands, I've spent some time wondering—"

But at that moment Greta brought in a silver teapot

and the subject was dropped. Nor was Charles's name mentioned by either of them again.

At the Contessa's request, Dinah poured out the tea and over the pleasant little meal they talked about Alpenglühen, the hotel and the Bergers.

"They are splendid people," the Contessa remarked appreciatively. "Honest, hard-working and kindly. The little Frau is a special friend of mine. We are both English by birth, you see, and if she sometimes feels a little homesick, she comes to me and we talk about the things we remember and love in our own country. That way, she gets it out of her system without hurting the feelings of that nice husband of hers!"

"She's lucky to have you for a confidant," Dinah said with a hint of wistfulness. "Do you live here all the time?"

"Most of it, particularly of late," the Contessa replied "You see, it has a very special place in my heart. My husband and I lived here for the last year of his life and I have very many happy memories—" She fell silent as if recalling some of those memories, but when she spoke again, there was no trace of sadness in her voice. "The view from this window is my favourite. Go and look out and you will see why."

Dinah obeyed and gave a little exclamation of delight. It was a perfect picture. Snow-clad mountains made the backcloth for a breathtaking view of the little valley below and in the clear air one could easily pick out individual buildings and even people. The hotel was easily distinguished, and even as she looked, Dinah saw Charles come out of it and exchange a few words with Emil as he went in.

"It is beautiful, isn't it?" the Contessa said. "And not only now. You should see it in the spring and summer. So green and fresh and friendly!"

"I'd like to see it then," Dinah said sincerely as she turned from the window.

"Perhaps you will, one day," the Contessa suggested, and seemed to check herself hurriedly. "And this room? Do you like it? I spend much of my time in it."

"It's beautiful," Dinah replied warmly. "And very

53

much *your* room, Contessa! I mean, it makes such a perfect background for you that I think it was designed and furnished especially for you, wasn't it?"

"As a matter of fact, it was," the Contessa confirmed, looking pleased. "My husband planned and chose every-. thing himself as a birthday surprise for me. He even designed that display cabinet for all my *bibelots*—" She indicated the handsome bow-fronted cabinet in which a host of tiny objects glinted in the diffused lighting with which it was fitted.

"May I look at them?" Dinah asked eagerly, and receiving permission, saw that against a background of beautiful, wide-spread fans the shelves were filled with the most attractive knick-knacks she had ever seen.

There were patch boxes of silver and gold, some of them decorated with precious stones. There were vinaig-rettes, one of them amusingly in the shape of a little fish. There were innumerable Japanese netsuki, exquisitely carved from ivory, jade and crystal. There were thumb-nail-sized singing birds in fragile cages and delicate little fans made from bird feathers or painted silk and mounted on wonderfully carved sticks. But what delighted Dinah most was the miniature furniture and household articles, mainly of silver, with which one shelf was filled. There were chairs and tables, none of which stood more than two inches high, some with even more fairylike cups and saucers and coffee pots arranged on them. There were rocking chairs, a little sedan chair complete with bearers, innumerable lamps and candlesticks, toilet requisites, some fitted into the cases specially made for them—such a wealth of lovely things that Dinah was bewildered and said so.

"They must have taken you a long time to collect!"

"Not as long as you might suppose," the Contessa explained. "I had the nucleus of the collection—quite a small one—before my marriage. Then for a few years, my husband and I travelled a lot, and we invariably found something to add to what I already had. Friends were very generous, too. Open the door, Dinah—it isn't locked—and take out anything you would like to look at more closely."

Dinah opened the door and after a moment's hesitation, carefully took out something which she found particularly fascinating. It was a silver Cinderella coach drawn by six prancing horses. A sturdy coachman sat on the box of the coach, and behind standing on their narrow platform, were two footmen. It was a work of art, for every detail, down to the tassels on the corners of the seat cushions and the tiny handles which turned to open the doors, was quite perfect. Yet to Dinah, there was an additional attraction.

"You know," she said in a puzzled way, "this seems familiar to me—though I've no idea why. I suppose I might have seen something similar in an antique shop, though I can't remember when or where."

"That was the very first piece I acquired," the Contessa said in an oddly strained voice. "It was given to me by my godfather on my twenty-first birthday and it fired the ambition in me to begin collecting."

"I'm not surprised," Dinah said fervently. "It's quite, quite beautiful."

None the less, she replaced the little treasure on its shelf, closed the door of the cabinet and came back to the Contessa's couch.

"Contessa, I think perhaps you're feeling a little bit tired, aren't you? she said diffidently. "Would you like me to go now?"

"No, no, my dear, not yet!" The Contessa caught at her hand and held it with surprising strength. "I'm really quite all right, I do assure you. Sit down, won't you, and talk to me. Tell me a little about yourself."

Despite her very real liking for the Contessa and the conviction that it was genuine interest and not just idle curiosity which prompted the request, Dinah was conscious of a feeling of withdrawal.

"There's really very little to tell," she began in a brittle voice. "I'm over here for a holiday—by myself," she added with a sudden touch of defiance.

But the Contessa took the announcement in her stride. "Why not?" she said calmly. "Particularly if your parents don't mind—"

"I have no parents," Dinah told her in a voice devoid

of all emotion. "And to all intents and purposes, I never have had. It was only about four years ago that my father died, but he was always too busy to want to see me. I spent all my time either at a boarding school or, sometimes, at the homes of other girls. Never with him!"

"And—your mother?"

"I know nothing whatever about my mother," Dinah replied bleakly. "Except that she left my father—and me—when I was about four years old. She may be alive for all I know, but since, in all these years, she's never tried to get in touch with me—" she broke off, biting her lip. "Forgive me, Contessa, but I'd rather not talk about it. I do my best to forget, but talking about it—" she swallowed convulsively.

"I shouldn't have asked you," the Contessa's voice shook. "It was impertinent of me—forgive me!'

"There's nothing to forgive," Dinah said quickly. "You couldn't possibly have known and—and I think if you don't mind, I'd better go now."

"Yes—" the Contessa agreed faintly. "Perhaps it would be better—"

For a moment Dinah stood looking down at the Contessa. Her eyes were closed and she was very pale. She looked much older and very, very tired. A wave of compassion engulfed Dinah. However much it hurt to speak of her lonely childhood, she ought not to have distressed this frail woman who had shown her so much kindness with her own bitterness. It was an unforgivable thing to have done.

She hesitated and then, acting on a sudden impulse, bent and kissed the pale cheek. The Contessa neither spoke nor opened her eyes, though Dinah thought she relaxed slightly. None the less, she was thankful that at that moment, Greta came in for the tea tray.

"I—I think the Contessa is very tired," Dinah said, and with a glance at her mistress Greta muttered something in German which Dinah didn't understand, though the look the maid gave her made it very clear that she wasn't wanted.

Dinah was in a depressed frame of mind when she

got back to the hotel. She had thoroughly enjoyed her visit up to the point when the Contessa had wanted to know more about her. After that, her pleasure vanished and in its place the pain of recalling her parents indifference had raged in its place.

Nor was it only that which troubled her. As she had told the Contessa, she had tried very hard to forget the past and thanks to her new-found happiness that Nicky's love had brought her, she had thought she had succeeded simply because it wasn't so important as it had been. Now she knew that she had been wrong. The old pain was still there, pushed into the background, but none the less lurking, ready to pounce at any unguarded moment.

And it was her own fault.

"I shouldn't have said so much," she said wretchedly. "I should just have told her that they were dead and left it at that. She wouldn't have probed any deeper if she'd seen that I didn't want her to. But somehow, I *had* to tell her! And as a result, I don't suppose I'll ever be asked to go there again—not that I'm sure I want to. Oh *dear*, why did it have to end like this?"

She cheered up when Nicky, who was in the foyer, came towards her.

"Hallo, darling, had a nice time?" he asked smilingly.

Dinah pulled herself together quickly. Not for the world did she intend to tell Nicky of that final scene. For one thing, it wasn't fair to unburden her woes at his expense, and for another, she knew that the more she dwelt on that old grief, the less she would be able to enjoy her present happiness.

"Very nice indeed," she told him, and then, because that didn't sound very convincing to her critical ears, she added hastily: "She's such a very charming, interesting person, and the Chalet is quite lovely."

"Then why were you walking as if you were unhappy?" Nicky asked astutely. "Oh yes, you were! Your shoulders were all hunched up and your feet were positively dragging. You looked as dispirited as if you'd lost a pound and picked up a penny! So what *is* the matter?"

"Well, I was thinking about the Contessa," Dinah confessed. "And—and feeling sad for her because she's so frail and yet so—so gallant. I think she's not nearly as well as she makes out—" her voice trailed away. That was the truth, so far as it went, but it was just another of those half-truths which she hated telling Nicky and yet which seemed so inevitable.

"And that's been one too many for your tender little heart," Nicky said gently, and went on masterfully: "I think, Dinah, I shall have to tell you that you're not to go and see her again. I'm sorry she's not well, but I can't have you upset like this!"

Dinah was about to protest, but Nicky continued speaking.

"Besides, I need you here!" He sounded half amused, half vexed. "To protect me. Oh yes, I mean that! I've been near to being kidnapped in the last half-hour!"

"Nicky!" she exclaimed incredulously.

"Oh, not in the sense of being held to ransom," he explained. "I suppose vamped would be a better word! You see, an American family has arrived—mother, father and daughter. And of all predatory little minxes, the girl takes the biscuit! She didn't wait for an introduction. She simply caught hold of my hand, paid me a fulsome compliment or two and announced that we were going to be the best of buddies! Honestly, Dinah, I was as petrified as a bird that's fascinated by a snake! If her mother hadn't called her at that moment to unpack, I don't know what would have happened by now. Still—" he went on more cheerfully, "once she knows what a lowly place I occupy in the scheme of things, she'll lose interest, thank heaven! I can't imagine her being permanently interested in anything less than a millionaire—multi-millionaire," he amended.

"Is she pretty?" Dinah asked, though she knew the answer to that! No girl who wasn't very pretty indeed would have such self-assurance as this one evidently had!

"See for yourself!" Nicky muttered with an upward glance at the landing, and almost ran to the sanctuary of the office and the protection of Frau Emil.

58

A girl ran lightly downstairs and involuntarily Dinah caught her breath. The newcomer had everything! She had short curly black hair and very dark expressive eyes set in a piquant little face. She was a tiny thing, hardly up to Dinah's eye level, but her slim body was beautifully proportioned and had a certain lusciousness about it. But she had more than that. She had charm. It radiated from her. The charm of confident youth and boundless vivacity. Irresistibly fascinating, it seemed to Dinah.

The girl came straight up to her, smiling as if quite sure of her welcome.

"Hallo!" she said in a soft, husky voice. "I'm Babette Vallaise, though mostly I'm called Bébé. Who are you?"

"Dinah Sherwood," for the life of her Dinah couldn't put any expression into her voice. "You've just come, haven't you?"

"And that puts me in my place!" Babette remarked, screwing her face up into a most attractive grimace. "You mustn't mind my impulsive ways, honey! It's the way I'm made. When I take to anybody, I just have to tell them right away! Which reminds me, who's that gorgeous Norse god you were talking to?"

"Mr. Gisborne," Dinah had no choice but to tell her. "He's the skiing instructor at the local club."

"Is that so!" Babette didn't look in the least disconcerted at the news. In fact, her eyes narrowed speculatively. "In that case, I'll certainly be wanting lessons! That can be arranged, I suppose?"

"Oh yes, you can buy his time," Dinah told her dryly, and instantly despised herself for having made such a paltry remark. It belittled both Nicky and herself.

Babette, however, didn't take it that way. From the way in which her dark eyes snapped, she took it as a challenge. Not that she said so. She didn't need to. She simply smiled confidently, even with amusement, and Dinah got the message. This preposterous girl quite genuinely believed that no man to whom she took a fancy would be able to resist her, and it amused her that anyone could be so dumb as not to appreciate the fact!

Charles *had* received an invitation from the Contessa, but just as in Dinah's case, he kept the fact to himself, though, unlike her, he was not too pleased at having received it. True, in the short time that he had been in the Contessa's company, he had felt considerably attracted to her, but the whole purpose of his holiday had been the need to be free of ties of any sort, and he felt a little put out since good manners made it impossible for him to excuse himself.

Yet by the time he reached the Chalet the following day, he felt more reconciled. The sunshine was glorious, the air as stimulating as wine and the view, as he climbed higher, increasingly beautiful. He himself was fitter than he had felt for years. To give an hour or so of his time to an elderly, ailing woman wasn't, after all, such a hardship.

None the less, as soon as he saw the Contessa, he knew that the visit was going to be a considerable strain. He had known, of course, that she was a sick woman, but he wasn't prepared for so great a change for the worse in her. There was a greyness about her face, a fluttering quality in the way she breathed which all too clearly told their own story. But it was her eyes that troubled him most. He had not remembered that they were so deeply set, or that they had burned with such devastating pain.

Yet when she spoke, her voice still had that warm, sweet quality which he had found so charming and it seemed perfectly natural to bend deferentially over the slender hand she held out to him.

"How very kind of you to come, Mr. Ravenscroft!"

"It gives me great pleasure to have done so," Charles said simply, and to his own surprise, meant it.

The Contessa smiled faintly, but she didn't reply, and Charles, realising that she was deliberately husbanding her strength, exerted himself to speak of trivialities in a leisurely, undemanding way which called for little more effort on his hostess's part than an occasional "Yes" or "No".

Greta brought the tea in, stayed to pour out and then quietly left, though not before she had looked anxiously at her mistress and then warningly at Charles.

The Contessa ate nothing though she drank thirstily. Once or twice she looked searchingly at Charles.

"She's wondering if she can trust me in some way or other," he told himself. "But why me—a stranger? Unless, of course—"

And as if in answer to his thought, the Contessa broke the silence between them with the one question above all which he had hoped she would not ask.

"Mr. Ravenscroft, you are a doctor, aren't you?"

"What makes you think that?" Charles parried lightly.

A momentary glimmer of amusement touched the Contessa's eyes.

"I've had far too much to do with members of your profession in the last few years not to be able to recognise the signs," she explained. "But don't worry, I've no intention of consulting you professionally or of discussing my health. But there is a very personal matter which is causing me considerable anxiety, and you may, if you're willing, be able to set my mind at rest, at least to some degree." She paused and then went on slowly: "So, you see, it's very reassuring to know that you are a member of a profession which knows how to keep a confidence."

"None the less, I'm a stranger to you," Charles warned. "And a confidence once given cannot be recalled. Are you quite sure—?"

"Quite sure," the Contessa assured him steadily. "I believe it's possible that you may be able to give me information which could enable me to right a great wrong —and as I haven't very much time at my disposal— yes—" as Charles looked keenly at her. "Just that! They give me another six months of life at the very outside."

There was no self-pity in the way she said it. No fear, either. Death might even come as a friend, he thought.

61

With a spontaneity which surprised him, Charles took her hand in his and held it firmly.

"I will do whatever I can to help you," he said quietly, and felt a slight responsive movement of the hand he held.

"I want you to tell me all you can about little Dinah Sherwood," she told him.

Charles looked at her in surprise. He hadn't known what was in her mind of course, but he certainly hadn't expected this.

"But, my dear Contessa, I know so little about Miss Sherwood," he protested. "My acquaintance with her dates only from when I arrived here a week or so ago."

"None the less—" the Contessa urged.

Charles frowned perplexedly. He would have to be careful—

"About her personal circumstances, I can tell you nothing, for we're not on confidential terms," he began slowly. "Indeed, until we were united in a common desire to be of assistance to you, there was considerable animosity between us."

Again that attractive glint of amusement enlivened the Contessa's eyes.

"Hardly surprising," she commented dryly. "*She* has red hair. *You* have a very determined chin. I should have been surprised if you hadn't clashed temperamentally!" She pondered. "By personal circumstances, do you mean that you know nothing about her family—or of her financial situation?"

"Nothing whatever," Charles declared firmly.

"But about Dinah herself," the Contessa asked insistently. "What sort of girl is she?"

"My first impression of her was that she was the happiest person I'd ever seen," he said thoughtfully. "My second, that she was a troublesome young termagant who needed a good spanking!"

The Contessa gave a soft little crow of laughter.

"And did you administer it, Mr. Ravenscroft?"

Charles grinned responsively.

"Only verbally, I do assure you, Contessa!"

62

"What a pity! Still, I suppose it wouldn't have done on such a short acquaintance. But what really interests me is why she should have attacked you—also verbally, no doubt. What had upset her?"

"She took exception to something I said to another guest," Charles told her briefly.

"And flew to his defence," the Contessa nodded. "For it was a man, of course. That handsome creature she was with at the Schokoladehaus?"

"Yes," Charles admitted even more briefly.

"I see." The Contessa sounded dissatisfied by his lack of response. "Mr. Ravenscroft, will you please tell me all about that incident? Believe me, I wouldn't ask you if I didn't think it could be important that I should know."

Charles stood up and walked over to the window. For several moments he stood staring out of it in silence. Then he turned and went back to the sofa.

"Contessa, you're putting me in a quandary," he told her gravely. "You see, while I would like to fall in with your wishes, I'm quite sure it would be very much better if the whole affair was forgotten. I hope you won't take it amiss when I tell you that, at the moment, I can see no reason why I should tell you any more about it than I already have."

He paused, but the Contessa made no reply and after a moment he went on quietly:

"You see, while I appreciate that you have taken a sincere liking for Miss Sherwood, I do find your interest in her rather extreme in view of the fact that, so far as I know, she is as much of a stranger to you as I am. Frankly, I would prefer to say no more—unless, of course—" he paused expectantly.

"Unless I can justify what at present seems to you to be no more than unreasonable curiosity?" the Contessa suggested. "Yes, I see your point, Mr. Ravenscroft. And I think I can do that to your satisfaction. You see—" she drew a deep breath, "I am—Dinah's mother!"

CHAPTER FOUR

DINAH'S mother! So that was it! No wonder, Charles thought, that he'd felt there was something familiar about the Contessa's eyes! They were Dinah's eyes, older, wiser, sadder, but unmistakably the same. Just why the sight of Dinah at the Schokoladehaus had been such a shock, however, was not so clear.

"Does Dinah know?" he asked, unconscious that, for the first time, he had referred to her by her Christian name.

"No," the Contessa said regretfully. "I had hoped that it would be possible for me to tell her yesterday when she was here, but I hadn't the courage."

Charles said nothing. He would not have been human if his curiosity hadn't, by now, become thoroughly aroused, yet he could not bring himself to ask questions. The Contessa, however, saved him from the necessity of doing that.

"Since I want your help, Mr. Ravenscroft, it's only right that I should explain the situation fully to you," she announced firmly.

"Of course, if that's what you wish," Charles replied. "But if, for a moment, I may speak to you as a doctor, I think it would be better if you were to postpone that for another occasion. I will willingly come back again tomorrow, if you would like that, but for the moment, I do advise you to rest."

"No, no," the Contessa said impatiently. "I can't do that until you do know. It won't take long—"

"Very well," Charles agreed, knowing that an argument could easily be more exhausting than letting her have her way would be.

For a moment the Contessa was silent as if she was marshalling her thoughts. Then she began slowly:

"I have been married twice. Dinah is my daughter by

my first marriage. Her father was Esmond Sherwood. Ah, you've heard of him?"

"Yes, indeed," Charles said with very real respect. "No one of my profession could fail to know of him. He was, and still is, the greatest authority on his subject the world has ever known, and his research work has undoubtedly saved the lives of countless people."

"Yes, I believe that to be absolutely true," the Contessa agreed gravely. "And yet, strangely, it was the desire for supremacy which spurred him on, never the thought of the people whose life he helped to save. They were simply a means to an end—little more to him than the animals he experimented on in his laboratory. That's a terrible thing to say of any human being. For a wife to say it of her husband must seem to you quite unpardonable, but for you to understand, I must say it. He had neither humility nor humanity, as I was to discover shortly after I married him." She pressed her lips closely together for a moment. "I need not go into detail about that except to say that he was not a man who should ever have married, and I don't think he would have done but for the fact that, with increasing fame, he had to entertain on a scale which made a hostess a necessity."

"But why did *you* marry *him*?" Charles asked, and the Contessa raised her hands in a gesture of exasperation.

"He was a very handsome man in an austere way. And he was, even then, a very important one. I was young and silly and I was flattered that such a man should want me for his wife." She paused. "Then Dinah was born. By then, my husband and I were almost completely estranged, but you must believe me, Mr. Ravenscroft, when I say that none the less, I hoped that our child would make a new bond between us. I was wrong. Esmond had no more use for her than he had for me. After a time, I was glad of that! She was mine, mine alone, and I told myself that I was completely happy. Then I met Guido Farini and I knew what happiness— and love—really were. None the less, we were not lovers. Something held us back. Dinah, perhaps, or the conviction that what we felt for one another was too precious to be sullied by vulgar intrigue. Guido went away and we didn't see one another for two years. Dinah was four by then. Then he came to see me and I knew at once that there was something terribly wrong. He told me. He had an incurable disease which would inevitably cause his death within a few years. That made a difference. How could we waste the precious time that was left to us? So I went away with him, and I took Dinah with me."

She covered her eyes with one hand and when she spoke again, it was in such a muted voice that Charles had to lean forward to hear.

"Esmond started divorce proceedings at once—I think he was probably glad to be rid of me. And I took it for granted that he would be equally indifferent to losing Dinah. I was wrong. He insisted on me giving her up entirely—oh, he was legally in the right, she had been put into his custody, but—but—" Her voice trailed away to silence.

Charles looked at her anxiously. She was, he was sure, almost on the point of collapse, but he was equally sure that nothing he could do or say would keep her from going through with what she had set herself to do. None the less—

He had noticed that on a side table there was a decanter of wine and an inverted glass. Now he went to it and half filled the glass. He brought it over to the Contessa and proffered it in silence. She sipped gratefully from it and Charles was relieved to see the faint colour return to her pale cheeks.

"Better," she told him, holding out the glass.

Charles took it and waited in silence. After a moment or so she went on :

"After the divorce, Guido and I were married, and we were very happy despite the threat which hung over us. Actually, we were luckier than we had dared to hope. We had five golden years together. Indeed, there was only one thing which marred our complete happiness. From the day on which I parted with Dinah to that morning when I saw her in the Schokoladehaus, I had never set eyes on her."

"No?" Charles said, considerably startled. "But she must have changed a lot in the interval. How was it that you were able to recognise her?"

"I'll tell you," the Contessa said eagerly. "When Dinah was little, Esmond not only refused to let me see her. He kept her hidden away so well that I was never able to find out where she was. But when she was old enough to go to school, by sheer coincidence, a very dear friend of mine sent her daughter to the same boarding school which Esmond had selected for Dinah. Fortunately the two girls became good friends, and since Esmond knew nothing of my friendship with Nina, it was possible for Dinah to be asked to visit when Ellen and she were on holiday. Of course, I didn't dare try to see her lest Esmond should find out and send her to another school. But I did have the satisfaction of knowing that Nina would keep a friendly eye on her. As well as that, she gave me news of Dinah and from time to time, sent me photographs of her."

"I see," Charles nodded. "But your first husband died some years ago, didn't he?"

"So why didn't I get in touch with Dinah then? Because I was afraid to," the Contessa confessed. "You see, I was quite sure that I would have only one chance to make my peace with Dinah, never a second. People of Dinah's age are so very positive in all they do and feel. To them, there's nothing between the whiteness of snow and the blackness of jet. And she had been so badly hurt, I didn't want to risk hurting her still more. So I did nothing until this trouble—" she laid her hand lightly over her heart—"became so intrusive that even before I was told, I knew that time was running out."

She paused again, her breath coming in uneven, shallow gasps. Charles picked up the wine glass again, but this time the Contessa shook her head.

"No, I've nearly finished." She took a grip on herself in a way which suggested she was relying on will power rather than on real strength.

"With Nina's help, we contrived that Dinah and I should be in Alpenglühen at the same time. We thought it might be possible to arrange an apparently unpremeditated meeting so that Dinah might get to know me and even, perhaps, learn to like me a little before I told her the truth. Even so, I hesitated to take the first step, but chance took it for me. The rest of the story you know, Mr. Ravenscroft."

"Not entirely, I think," Charles said thoughtfully. "Dinah was attracted to you from the first. She told me so herself. And since that first meeting she has visited you here. On the face of it, your plans have developed even better than you could have hoped. Yet now you're considerably distressed. So what went wrong, Contessa?"

"I was too impatient," she confessed. "I asked her questions about herself in too direct a way—and despite her liking for me, which she didn't try to hide, she shrank into herself and I knew that I'd lost any ground that I might have gained. Oh, if only I'd waited!"

"It might have been wiser," Charles acknowledged. "And frankly, it seems to me that you were behaving so out of character that there can be only one explanation for that. So I conclude that, quite apart from the question of your health, there's some other reason why it seemed such a matter of urgency for you to establish the relationship as soon as possible. Young Gisborne, of course."

"Yes, Mr. Gisborne." The Contessa hesitated. "I suppose every mother, particularly the mother of a daughter, is over-anxious about their choice of a life partner. And Dinah, I'm reasonably sure, has, because of her past history, an inevitable weakness. She is more than usually sensitive to kindness. To her, being wanted and loved is the most important thing in life. Is it surprising that I should be concerned lest her feelings for Mr. Gisborne are more a question of being in love with love than the genuine article?"

"I'm afraid I'm no authority on such matters," Charles told her, hedging a little because he didn't altogether like the way the conversation was heading.

"But I should have thought it quite likely that her feelings for Gisborne will either turn into the genuine article—or else will gradually fade away."

"So, either way, why worry?" the Contessa suggested. "Because, Mr. Ravenscroft, Dinah is of age and of independent means. There is nothing to prevent them from getting married at once—before she has had time to get to know what Mr. Gisborne is really like. *That's* what worries me, because so much depends on it." She hesitated. "I have already been given some information about the young man. It was not reassuring, but in fairness, I have to admit that it comes from a prejudiced source—"

Frau Emil? Charles wondered. Could be. It would fit in, and it would explain several other things which had puzzled him.

"What I want from you, Mr. Ravenscroft," the Contessa went on with almost feverish urgency, "is the unbiased opinion of a man who knows something of the world. Will you do that for me?"

It seemed to Charles that quite suddenly a warning light flashed into his brain. Not for a moment did he disbelieve the Contessa's story, which had aroused his very real sympathy. Nor did he doubt that her anxiety on Dinah's behalf was both genuine and understandable. And yet—

The Contessa was a very sick woman who knew that her span of life was limited and professional knowledge and experience had taught Charles that in such circumstances, judgment could become warped. Not only did anxieties become exaggerated, but almost any action seemed justified, however reckless, if it seemed to offer a solution. And already, the Contessa had admitted that her impatience had been a mistake. Now, that tense urgency told Charles quite unmistakably that she had not learned her lesson. Even now she could see only her own point of view, and though she no doubt fully intended that anything he told her about Nicky Gisborne would be in the strictest confidence, she might well forget that and make use of it in the future if that seemed to her to be advisable. That, with all its possibly embarrassing consequences, Charles was not prepared to risk. He must make a stand—now.

"I'm afraid it's too late for me to do that," he said pleasantly but with unmistakable firmness. "You see, like most men, I have an ingrained prejudice against extreme good looks in other members of my own sex. It's no doubt unreasonable since looks are a matter of luck, not choice. But there it is. So, though I'm sorry to appear disobliging, I'm just not in a position to help you. My opinion would not be unbiased." He stood up with the intention of making it clear that the last word had been said. "Do forgive me, Contessa!"

"There's nothing to forgive," the Contessa assured him quietly. "On the contrary, I must thank you for having listened so patiently to me. Having put my anxieties into so many words has clarified my mind as to exactly what they are. And that is always helpful."

"I'm glad," Charles said automatically.

But that wasn't true. On his way back to the hotel, he felt anything but satisfaction. Sick or not, the Contessa had a very shrewd brain and he had the uneasy feeling that by refusing to discuss Nicky Gisborne he had, in fact, betrayed his opinion of that young man almost as completely as if he had given the Contessa chapter and verse for his dislike and lack of trust. To say nothing was the equivalent of admitting that there was nothing to be said in praise.

Yet what else could he have done? At least, even if she did read between the lines, she couldn't quote him as having said anything of a detrimental nature. That was something!

People! Especially women! Heavens, how they cluttered up life and made it difficult to concentrate on really important things! Well, at least he had been warned never to let himself be cornered again as he had been just now. It might even be a good idea to cut his holiday short—

"He had neither humility nor humanity—"

He jerked the thought of the Contessa's words away impatiently. Natural enough, no doubt, for her to regard her first husband in that light, but he, Charles, with his deeper appreciation of the value of Esmond Sherwood's work, could easily understand just how demanding that work must have been.

The Contessa had, of course, been right when she had said that Sherwood was a man who should never have married. There was no place for such trivialities in his life. And that, surely, was a warning to any man whose work was a vocation in the most demanding sense of the word. To himself, in fact.

Well, he had already decided not to contemplate marriage until his feet were very firmly set on the ladder of success. Might it not be even more to the point to leave it out of his plans altogether?

After all, he travels fastest who travels alone—

Dinah looked up expectantly from the magazine she had been idly thumbing through as Charles came into the hotel foyer. Thanks to a minor ankle injury that morning on the slopes she had had a thoroughly boring and uncomfortable afternoon. But Nicky had said that, with any luck, he would be able to get back earlier than usual, so she had settled herself here in order to be able to greet him as soon as he arrived. But time was getting on and still he hadn't come. Now, as she saw that the newcomer wasn't Nicky but Charles, her disappointment made it impossible to greet him with anything more than a casual nod of the head. Charles, fortunately, didn't seem to notice, for his response was equally brief and impersonal. Indeed, Dinah received the vague impression that there was something almost defensive in his manner. If anything, she was relieved. In her present mood the last thing she wanted was to have to make polite conversation.

However, just as Charles reached the foot of the stairs, Frau Emil came out of the office and intercepted him.

"Oh, Mr. Ravenscroft, how did you find the Contessa?" she asked anxiously.

So Charles *had* been invited to the Chalet! Involuntarily Dinah pricked up her ears to hear Charles's reply, but it wasn't at all informative.

"Oh, much as usual, I should think," he said vaguely, but also with a hint of surprise at the question.

Frau Emil coloured slightly, evidently feeling that Charles thought she was speaking out of turn.

"You must forgive my interest," she said quietly. "But, you see, the Contessa has been very kind to me. Like me, she is English, and sometimes, if I get homesick, she lets me go to the Chalet and talk to her."

"I quite understand," Charles said politely, but he added no more to what he had already said.

There was a brief, awkward silence. Then Frau Emil, clearly not wishing to appear inquisitive, changed the subject abruptly.

"Miss Sherwood has had some bad luck," she remarked breathlessly. "She injured her ankle this morning."

"Oh?" Charles turned to Dinah. "Not badly, I hope?" he asked Dinah without any evidence of interest.

"Fortunately, no," she replied curtly, determined not to appear to be asking for sympathy. "A day or two's rest will put it right."

"Good," Charles said casually, and with a very slight nod which included them both, continued on his way upstairs.

Again there was a brief, uneasy silence. Then Frau Emil said hurriedly :

"Well, I must get on with it ! I've a lot to do !"

And Dinah was again alone—but not for long. Again the door swung open and Nicky came in—but not alone. Bébé Vallaise was with him. She looked quite stunning. The scarlet outfit she was wearing suited her dark colouring to perfection, but it was her vivid, intriguing little face that riveted Dinah's attention. Obviously she was in the highest of spirits, and something she had just said had evidently amused Nicky, for he was laughing appreciatively. Indeed, so absorbed were they in their conversation that neither appeared so much as to notice Dinah until, with a little cry, Bébé came to an abrupt halt by her chair.

"Oh, Dinah, I didn't notice you !" she said with such excessive sweetness that it was perfectly clear to Dinah that what she was really saying was: *"Nicky didn't notice you!"*

Nicky must have realised that, too, for he said:

"Dinah, my dear!" very quickly and sat down beside her. "How is the ankle now?"

"Quite a bit better," Dinah assured him untruthfully, since it seemed to have started throbbing violently again in the last few moments. "But I'm afraid it will take a day or two to mend completely!"

"Hard luck!" Bébé said in her soft, husky voice. And then, with a casual: "See you in the bar," to Nicky, she ran upstairs.

For a moment neither Dinah nor Nicky spoke. Then he laughed—a laugh that, conflictingly, held both irritation and amusement.

"That girl!"

"Oh, has she been—difficult?" Dinah asked cautiously.

"Difficult? Impossible!" Nicky declared explosively. "But for her I'd have been back an hour ago! But no, when she heard that I'd got a spare period following her lesson, she insisted that we carried on."

"How—awkward," Dinah said, again choosing her words with care.

And she appeared to have said the right thing, for Nicky's face cleared and he gave her hand a little squeeze.

"Awkward is right!" he said feelingly. "I knew you'd understand, Dinah. I'd have given anything to have told her that there was nothing doing, but how could I? The Club employs me to be at the beck and call of the members, and I'd have been in hot water if she'd complained that I was shirking my job."

"You think she would have complained?" Dinah said tentatively.

"I'm darned well certain she would have done," Nicky said unhesitatingly. "She's been brought up to believe that money can buy anything if you offer enough, and if anyone suggests that it can't, she simply offers more until she does get her own way. Why, would you believe it, when I told her that I intended knocking off an hour earlier she promptly offered me double rates to carry on!" he concluded indignantly.

"But you didn't accept?" Dinah asked quickly.

"Good lord, no! What do you take me for?" Nicky replied reproachfully. "My job may not be a very exalted one, but I have got some pride left! I don't accept tips or bribes—least of all from snippets like our Miss Vallaise!"

"No, of course not," Dinah agreed, but her heart sank. How she wished she had not made that spiteful remark to Bébé Vallaise about being able to buy Nicky's time! Evidently it had rankled, and Bébé had taken the first available opportunity to demonstrate that even though it was true, at least she didn't have to pay over the odds for it, which was something of a consolation to her, no doubt. But not, Dinah was sure, so much as the fact that she had been able to persuade Nicky to give up his plan to get back early to the hotel.

"Did you tell her why you wanted to get off early?" she asked apprehensively.

"No, I didn't, though judging by what she said, she may have guessed," Nicky admitted, scowling. "Something about absence making the heart grow fonder—" he looked at his watch. "Just time for a drink before we go up to change. How about it?"

Dinah agreed, and holding on to Nicky's arm limped painfully to the bar. She sat down at one of the little tables while Nicky got the drinks. He was rather a long time since there were a good many other people waiting to be served and he had only just set the glasses down on their table when Bébé arrived. Nicky swore softly under his breath, but after pausing dramatically in the doorway to make sure that everyone was aware of her presence, she strolled over to join a group of laughing youngsters whose ranks quickly opened to welcome her. Of Nicky's and Dinah's presence she seemed to be completely oblivious.

And that, Dinah admitted unwillingly, was clever of her. First she had quite deliberately set out to make Nicky feel flattered by the way she had sought his company so blatantly. Now she was bestowing her

74

favours elsewhere so that he couldn't be sure of himself! Clever, yes, but contemptible!

Not that it really mattered, for such feminine tactics had passed right over Nicky's head.

"Well, thank goodness for that!" he murmured fervently. "I was afraid she was going to do the porous plaster act for the rest of the evening. Another drink? Or would you rather go up to dress?"

"Go up, I think," Dinah decided. "With this ankle I expect I'll be rather slow."

"Fair enough." Nicky took the empty glasses back to the bar. To do so, he had to pass near to Bébé, who tossed him a casual, laughing remark. Whether Nicky replied Dinah couldn't tell since his back was towards her, but when he returned, he was obviously annoyed.

"It would give me the greatest pleasure in the world to put that girl across my knees and give her six of the best," he remarked irritably. "She's got a tongue like a viper!"

Dinah contented herself with a little wordless sound of sympathy, but once in her own room, she sat down on her bed and thought over the last half-hour, and what she thought was disturbing, to say the least of it.

Bébé Vallaise was a menace. Oh, not that for a moment Dinah thought that Nicky would succumb to her wiles. He had already made it perfectly clear that he thought she was a nuisance. But, if Dinah knew anything about girls of that type, that would only make her all the more determined to get what she wanted. And that, unmistakably, was Nicky's attention—even devotion.

So, whatever the outcome, it was a disastrous state of affairs for Nicky. Supposing, just for one horrible moment, that Bébé did beguile him into caring for her? Inevitably, Dinah knew, he would despise himself for his disloyalty to her and, in any case, there could be no lasting happiness for him, since Bébé was hardly likely really to care for him. It was simply that her vanity demanded that every personable male she met should find her more attractive than any other girl, but once she had broken down his resistance, she would quickly lose interest, and would pass on to her next conquest.

But all that passed only fleetingly through Dinah's mind, dismissed because she had perfect faith in Nicky's love and loyalty. What she had to worry about was what would happen when Bébé discovered that, for once in her life, she wasn't going to have her own way.

Dinah frowned over the problem. That either Mr. or Mrs. Vallaise would do anything to check their daughter, however outrageously she might behave, was out of the question. In their eyes, she could do no wrong and they would certainly play whatever part she wanted them to. Dinah couldn't see what that part might be, but she did appreciate that, with their help, Bébé was in a very strong position.

And Nicky, of course, was in a very weak one—and knew it. He had already made that clear when he'd said that he couldn't risk giving offence and having complaints made about him at the Club. As a result, Bébé had been able to prevent him from coming back to the hotel as early as he had wanted to. It was a small triumph but an ominous one.

Dinah bit her lip. Besides the fear of losing his job, Nicky faced another disadvantage. No decent man likes fighting a woman, and Nicky was no exception. However much he wanted to keep Bébé at arm's length, he would do his utmost to let her down as lightly as possible so that she didn't too obviously lose face.

"If only men realised that women are just as tough— if not tougher—than men when it comes to getting what they want," Dinah reflected regretfully. But depressing though the thought was, it suddenly gave her the answer she had been looking for. The only opponent a girl like Bébé had to fear was someone who knew instinctively how a woman's mind works, and who wasn't handicapped by the chivalrous feelings that beset a man. In other words, another woman. Herself.

"Why didn't I realise that before?" Dinah marvelled, and began to make plans.

To begin with, clothes. Bébé favoured brilliant colours that immediately attracted attention to her.

Her ski suit had been scarlet. The dress into which she had changed was a shocking pink—both colours that Dinah knew she couldn't possibly wear with her colour hair.

"But in any case, I don't want to copy her," she decided firmly. "That would be too obvious. But—"

She limped over to her wardrobe and surveyed its contents. Blues and greens predominated, though there were several pale yellow and deep, tawny brown dresses as well. Nothing very spectacular except—

She took out one dress and inspected it thoughtfully. It was a dress that she had never been quite sure she really liked, though she had let her friend, Ellen Joliffe, persuade her into buying it when they had gone on a shopping spree together in preparation for Dinah's holiday.

It was simply but beautifully cut in lines that, Dinah knew, moulded it closely to her supple figure. Rather too closely, in her opinion. But that wasn't the only reason why she hadn't been sure she liked it. The brilliance of the peacock blue-green material of which it was made seemed garish to her eyes and so far she hadn't had the courage to wear it. But now—

A little later, when she left her room, she had the satisfaction of knowing that, though in a different way, her appearance was quite as striking as Bébé's had been in her pink dress.

But her satisfaction was short-lived. As she closed the door behind her, another door a little way down the corridor opened and Bébé herself emerged. It was all that Dinah could do to restrain a startled gasp. Bébé was no longer wearing the pink dress. Instead, she had changed into one of deep midnight blue, so demurely cut as to appear almost Quakerish, an effect which was heightened by the stiff white ruching with which the neck was outlined.

"Hallo!" she drawled casually as she came level with Dinah. "Such a bore—Tommy Coats didn't look where he was going and he spilt his beer all over me! My dear, I simply *had* to change! I mean, the *smell* as well as being half drowned!" She grimaced expressively.

77

"How vexing!" Dinah said mechanically.

"Yes, wasn't it?" Bébé agreed—but she didn't sound in the least put out. On the contrary, Dinah had seen an unmistakable glint of amused triumph in the dark eyes and had little difficulty in interpreting it. Far from the luckless Tommy being responsible for an accident, she was quite sure that Bébé herself had deliberately contrived it.

And of course, the reason why she had done so was only too obvious. She had put on that pink dress with the express intention of spurring Dinah on to react in exactly the way that she had. Then, creating an excuse for changing, she had gone to the other extreme. As a result, Dinah not only felt unpleasantly overdressed and flashy. She felt frightened as well. Bébé had utterly out-manoeuvred her.

To Dinah's great relief, by the following morning her ankle was considerably better. Not only had the swelling gone down to a large extent, but it was far less painful. Frau Berger, wise in the experience of many such mishaps, assured her that she had nothing to worry about—if she was sensible.

"For it is rest and rest alone which you need," Frau Berger admonished. "And it is difficult when one is young and the sun is shining to accept idleness. But I tell you, I *know* that if you are foolish you will only make longer the time before you can venture on the snows again. Do you understand?"

"Yes—and I know you're right, Frau Berger," Dinah acknowledged. "But—" she sighed wistfully—"it does seem such a waste of time when—when I could be enjoying myself."

Frau Berger heard that little pause and guessed what it meant, for though she and her husband were content now to leave much of the hotel management to the younger generation, none the less, very little went on of which the older woman was in ignorance. She knew all about the lightning romance between this attractive girl and the very handsome young ski-instructor, and though it was not strictly any business of hers, she was

78

concerned on Dinah's account. One had, of course, to move with the times, but with all her motherly heart she wished that Dinah had not come here alone. She was too sensitive and too vulnerable to be without the protective presence of parents. Even today, that meant something, no matter how far their adventuresome fledglings might relegate them to the back seat, as Mr. and Mrs. Vallaise were firmly relegated. Ah, that girl! The Vallaise family were good spenders—and no one appreciated that quality in visitors more than Frau Berger. None the less, she could wish they hadn't come to the Tannenhof. For, without doubt, there was going to be trouble—trouble that might cause unhappiness to this nice little girl. But what could she do? True, Mrs. Joliffe, who had been responsible for Dinah coming here, had written asking her to keep an eye on her, but that gave her no authority, no right to advise, however tactfully. Still, one could perhaps help a little—

"Now, how are you going to amuse yourself today?" she asked kindly when she had finished her inspection of Dinah's ankle.

"Oh—" it was a question that Dinah had been asking herself and to which she had found no answer— "I've some letters to write. And that reminds me, Frau Berger, I had a letter from Ellen Joliffe a few days ago. She's getting married in a month or two and she wants me to be her chief bridesmaid. Oh—and her mother has asked me if, when I leave here, I'll go back to live with them and perhaps stay on after Ellen is married to—well, not to take Ellen's place, of course, but at least to keep Mrs. Joliffe company until she gets used to not having Ellen with her."

Frau Berger only just managed to repress a sigh of relief. So, in the not very distant future, the good Mrs. Joliffe would be taking the child under her kindly wing again! That was very good, yet it was the present —the immediate present—that was so dangerous. She would have liked to know just how much the Joliffes knew about Dinah's romance. Possibly the little Ellen was in her confidence, but the mother? That was another matter. The young had a sense of loyalty to one another which made them unwilling to divulge a confidence to the parent generation—

"That should be enjoyable for you," she said genially. "Preparing for a wedding is such excitement. So many plans, so much to do! But afterwards, for the mother who has been so busy, a loss of spirits. You will, I am sure, be a great comfort to her. It is a good plan!"

"Yes," Dinah agreed, because there was nothing else she could say without telling Frau Berger that with her own affairs in such an unsettled state, she was not at all sure that she would be able to fall in with Mrs. Joliffe's suggestion.

For Nicky had said nothing more about her money and the difficulties it raised in his mind since he had told her that he needed time to think things over. She told herself that she was being too impatient, but it was impossible not to feel anxious. Nicky was so moody these days—so different from the gay person he had been when they had first met.

Money! What a nuisance it could be, whether one had too much or too little! If only she had had more experience of the world—and of men in particular! But her upbringing in the seclusion of the school had prevented that, and even the time during which she had lived with the Joliffes hadn't been all that helpful because, with Ellen's gay assistance, she had tried to crowd in all the good times she had missed previously. There had been no time for serious thought.

What she felt she wanted was to be able to talk things over with an older, more experienced woman— Mrs. Joliffe, for instance, if only she was here. But she wasn't, and writing, Dinah was sure, wouldn't be as satisfactory. Almost she was tempted to take Frau Berger into her confidence, but something held her back from that, and when the Frau left a little later after having invited Dinah to have mid-morning coffee with her and her daughter-in-law, Dinah was left with her problem.

Nor was it ever far out of her mind in the next few days, for still Nicky said nothing, and the longer the time that passed, the less able Dinah felt to bring up the topic herself.

Then, quite suddenly, she realised that there was someone available in whom she felt she could safely confide. The Contessa! She, Dinah was quite sure, would be both understanding and helpful. If only she hadn't been so rude to the Contessa! Well, wasn't that all the more reason why she should go and see her? Apologise for her abrupt departure, and explain what had led to it? Surely the Contessa would forgive her and then it would be possible to ask her advice—yes, she would go this very afternoon. She would hire a car so that she didn't put too much strain on her ankle, of course.

It all seemed so simple, but it didn't work out as she had hoped. When she arrived at the Chalet it was to be met with the news that the Contessa had left for Italy the previous day to stay with relatives and had not said when she would be returning.

Disconsolately, Dinah returned to the hotel, convinced that now her plan had come to nothing, heartbreak must almost inevitably lie ahead.

Yet, later that day, she was thankful that she had not seen the Contessa, for, abruptly, Nicky broke the long silence that had overshadowed them both.

"Dinah, I've been thinking about—us," he told her in a queer, staccato voice.

Dinah's heart seemed to stop beating. She waited in silence, hardly breathing.

"It comes to this," Nicky went on. "I don't like the way things are. A man ought not to live on his wife's money. It's a situation that robs him of something— the feeling that he amounts to anything—that he's pulling his weight. And that's not just a question of vanity. It's something—basic, something that could be disastrous."

Dinah sat very still. So this was the end of it! Well, it hardly surprised her. But Nicky was saying something more. After what he had already said it couldn't be very important, but she forced herself to listen.

"Then I thought of what you said about giving your

money away. But I couldn't feel that was right either. I couldn't let you be subjected to the dreariness and discomfort that living on my pittance would mean." He drew a deep breath. "I felt as if I was up against a stone wall with no way through it. It seemed to me that the only thing was for us to part. But as soon as I'd come to that conclusion, I knew just how impossible it was. Dinah—" he put his hand under her chin and turned her face up to his—"I can't put you out of my life. You mean too much to me! So—" he squared his shoulders and when he spoke again, all sign of indecision had gone from his voice, "I'm asking you if you'll take a chance and marry me, though I'm warning you, I'm going to make one condition that you'll have to accept!"

CHAPTER FIVE

DINAH didn't hesitate.

"Nicky darling, of *course*!"

"But you haven't heard my condition yet," Nicky protested.

"I accept it—whatever it is. You wouldn't ask me to promise anything I ought not to," Dinah declared stoutly.

An expression that she couldn't interpret flickered momentarily in Nicky's eyes—and was gone.

"None the less, I want you to hear it, so that there can be no chance of misunderstanding afterwards," he said stubbornly. "So please listen, Dinah. It's just this— no matter how much money you've got, I want to *do* something—have a job of my own, I mean. A *real* job that takes an effort to hold it down. Oh, darling, don't look so hurt! Try to understand. It isn't just a question of—" he smiled wryly, "my masculine dignity! Quite honestly, having everything I want without lifting a finger to get it would drive me crazy! You see, though I know quite a lot of people wouldn't believe it, I'm not the playboy type. Oh, I don't mean to say I don't want to have a good time. Of course I do—who doesn't? But if life is one long holiday, it would bore me. It's the contrasts in life that make it exciting. The ups and downs, the hard work and *then* the holiday. Do you see what I'm getting at?" he ended anxiously.

"Yes, I do," Dinah said eagerly. "And I think you're quite right. It's something I've been thinking about quite a lot lately. Oh, not about you. About myself. You see, ever since I left school I've done nothing but play. I've tried to catch up for all the fun I didn't have as a child. I've enjoyed it tremendously, especially, of course, since I came here. But now—I know I want something more than just fun out of life, though I really don't know what," she confessed honestly. "But something worth while."

She looked so sweet and serious that, involuntarily, Nicky smiled as he drew her gently to him.

"Like taking me on as a husband—and making a real home for us to share?" he suggested softly. And then, as if the idea had only just occurred to him : "You know, Dinah, it's odd, but neither of us have ever had that. In my case, it wasn't my parents' fault. They were both stage people. I don't think I've ever told you that before. Because of it, they were so often on the move and they never had a settled home. In fact, I didn't see a great deal of them and when I did, it was at boarding houses or small hotels—neither of them exactly homelike."

"Oh, Nicky!" Dinah's eyes were very tender. "Yes, that will be the most worthwhile job of all! Of course," she went on reflectively, "I'll probably make mistakes because I know so little about what really makes a home."

"Are you so sure of that?" Nicky asked quizzically. "Isn't it more likely to be the case that because you missed so much, you'll know all the better what's really needed to make a real home?"

"The things that are more important than having a beautifully furnished home," Dinah said dreamily. "Things like love and trust and the knowledge that you're wanted. Yes, you're right, Nicky. Home ought to be the place that one enjoys being in most because it's possible to relax and be one's real self—"

"Something like that," Nicky agreed. "But don't get too lost in the future, darling. Let's live in the present for the moment!" He fumbled in his pocket and brought out a little ring case. "I hope you won't think I've taken too much for granted, Dinah, but I got this for you today—if you like to have it. It isn't nearly good enough for you, and one day, I'm going to replace it with something that is. But in the meantime, will you wear this for me?"

He opened the case and took out the ring. Dinah gave a little gasp of delight. Perhaps it hadn't cost a great deal, but none the less, it was extremely attractive, owing, perhaps, more to the setting than the stones, though the aquamarine centre stone had a beautiful depth of colour and the tiny diamonds which circled it sparkled bravely.

"Oh, how *beautiful*, Nicky!" Dinah declared fervently. "I'll *never* want another one to take its place!"

She held out her hand and Nicky slipped the ring on her finger. It fitted perfectly.

"It's as though it was made specially for me," Dinah breathed happily. "Oh, Nicky, I do love it, and I'll be so proud to wear it!"

Nicky lifted her hand to his lips in silence. Then, as their eyes met, he caught her close and kissed her with sudden passion.

"I only hope you'll never regret—" he muttered against her soft, responsive lips.

"I never shall," Dinah told him gravely. "I'm quite sure of that!"

But a strange restlessness seemed to overcome Nicky and his expression grew moody as he let her go.

"I hope to heaven you're right. But you know so little about me—you're taking an awful lot on trust, Dinah!"

"So are you, if it comes to that," Dinah told him spiritedly. "For all you know, I may be a mass of secret vices!"

Nicky's face cleared and he laughed.

"You absurd infant! Well, it sounds intriguing, to say the least of it! What sort of vices, may I ask? Are you a successful drug-pusher? Or a member of an international spy-ring? Or—I know! You're the master mind that's at the back of all the big bank robberies! That's it, isn't it?"

Dinah shook her head.

"I'm not going to tell you!" she announced provocatively. "It will be much more exciting for you to have to find out for yourself!"

Nicky looked at her with startled eyes. Then he laughed.

"So it will," he agreed lightly. "Well, let's leave that to the future and instead, let's have a drink to celebrate, shall we, my hardened criminal?"

"Yes, let's," Dinah agreed gaily, and lifted her hand to look again at her new treasure. "I wonder if anyone will notice?"

"I think they will," Nicky said a trifle drily. "Anyhow, let's find out."

He tucked his hand underneath her arm and so linked, they made their way to the bar. It was rather crowded and at first, in the crush, no one noticed Dinah's ring. Then, with a little squeal, Bébé pounced on her hand and held it up for everyone to see.

"Look, Momma! Look, Poppa!" She displayed Dinah's hand to her parents. "Isn't it lovely? Dinah, I do wish you every happiness!"

Her parents, taking their cue from her, added their good wishes. Then Nicky joined them and in a flash, Bébé turned on him.

"As for you, Nicky Gisborne, you're just the luckiest man in the world, because Dinah's the sweetest girl I've ever met!"

"Thanks, Bébé," Nicky said easily. "I quite agree with you. She is!" And again, smiling down at her, he tucked his hand possessively under Dinah's arm.

"Well, mind you never change your mind about that!" Bébé said with mischievous effrontery. "Because if you do, you'll have me to reckon with, and I can be fierce with anybody who doesn't play the game by my friends! And now—" she turned impulsively to her father. "Poppa, this is an occasion! Don't you think it calls for champagne?"

"Why, that's an idea, Bébé!" Mr. Vallaise beamed all over his keen, square-jawed face. He had thought his little girl had shown signs of being interested in young Gisborne herself, but either he had been wrong or else, if he was right, then Bébé was bluffing admirably. He approved of that. Never allow yourself to lose face by admitting that someone else has beaten you to it! It was a policy he had believed in all his life and it had always paid dividends. Sometimes, even, in the end, you got what you wanted after all! Well, in this case, time would show, and in the meantime, he was prepared to back his daughter to the limit!

He did it handsomely. It wasn't just champagne for his family and the newly engaged couple. It was champagne for everyone in the bar—late arrivals as well. And that included Charles.

A glass was thrust into his hand without explanation until Bébé, seeing his surprise, sidled towards him through the crowd.

"Dinah and Nicky have just announced their engagement, so we're drinking their health," she explained, lifting her own glass. "Won't you join in?"

"Certainly," Charles said equably. "I wish them every happiness—as I'm sure you do." And raising his glass, he clinked it against Bébé's before sipping from it.

Bébé's dark eyes snapped. And just what did that mean? Had he seen through her determined effort not to show the chagrin that was seething within her? Could be, with those dark, penetrating eyes of his. But if so, then she wasn't going to take him up on it as Nicky, so she had found out, had done on another occasion when Charles had made a remark which might have a *double entendre*. Nicky, she knew, had been the loser by doing that and she had no intention of making a similar mistake. None the less, it was something to remember.

"Well, come over and give them your good wishes in person," she said gaily, and catching hold of his hand, pulled him, willy-nilly, over to where Dinah and Nicky were standing—oddly enough, seeing that they were the reason for the celebration—alone.

Dinah, in particular, was feeling rather out of things. In some subtle way this had become the Vallaises' party of which she and Nicky were of no more importance than anyone else who was benefiting by the generosity of their host. As a result she gave Charles a warmer smile than she might otherwise have done and Charles found it easier to put genuine feeling into his good wishes than he had thought would be the case. Even Nicky forgot his previous antipathy and responded pleasantly.

For a few moments the four of them stood chatting.

Then, once again, Bébé took Dinah's hand and displayed the ring.

"Isn't it lovely?" she said with every sign of sincerity.

"It is, indeed," Charles agreed unhesitatingly.

"Particularly as aquamarines stand for faithfulness," Bébé added dreamily. Then, with a little smile, she let go of Dinah's hand and drifted off.

An uneasy silence followed her departure. Nicky was scowling and Dinah, only too well aware of the fact, felt tongue-tied and unhappy. It was Charles who stepped into the breach.

"I've often wondered how it has come about that stones are supposed to have special properties," he remarked lightly. "Some of them not too pleasant, either. Opals, for instance. But I really can't credit it that such a lovely thing can possibly be unlucky."

"Or that pearls mean tears," Dinah said rather breathlessly. "I suppose there could be a reason, though I think it's probably sheer superstition."

"Well, anyway, I know what *this* particular stone means," Nicky declared rather loudly, and lifted Dinah's hand to his lips. "That the girl I love has promised to marry me and that I'm the happiest man alive!"

Glancing across the room, Charles saw that Bébé had seen the gesture though she might not have heard the words which accompanied it. And this time, she could not hide her chagrin.

The next few days were among the happiest that Dinah had known since coming to Alpenglühen. In fact, everything seemed to conspire to make it that way.

Her ankle was quite better now and she was able to go out on to the ski slopes again, although Nicky insisted that she didn't overdo it.

"Better safe than sorry," he warned her. "Remember that, quite apart from your ankle, all your muscles have got a bit slack. Take it easy for a day or two and then you can really get going!"

And though Dinah was disappointed, that was more than compensated for by Nicky's care of her. Rather shyly she told him so, and Nicky looked pleased.

"So long as you do realise that it's because I want to look after you and not just that I'm trying to be bossy," he said.

Another thing had happened which gave Dinah both satisfaction and pleasure. Since the announcement of their engagement both Nicky and she seemed to have been accepted by the other visitors in a way that they hadn't been before. It meant that they were included in various groups where previously they had only been on the edge of them. To Dinah that was particularly pleasant, for it meant that while Nicky was busy and she had time on her hands, she no longer felt left out either at the hotel or the Club. As a result, she found that she had regained the self-confidence which had seemed to desert her since coming to Alpenglühen, and which even Nicky's devotion hadn't wholly restored.

But perhaps the most satisfactory thing that had happened was that Bébé had evidently accepted the significance of their engagement, and no longer exhibited any of that irritating possessiveness where Nicky was concerned. She was just pleasant and friendly towards both of them, and if her father was inclined to watch his daughter with slightly sardonic amusement, Dinah certainly didn't notice it, though Charles did— and wondered.

He had, in fact, quite a lot to wonder about these days where Bébé was concerned. For, with the utmost aplomb, she took him under her wing in a most maternal way, though she did treat him with a certain amount of deference. None the less, she insisted firmly that he ought to play a bigger part in all the available activities —particularly those which they could share. In vain Charles tried to get out of it, explaining that really he was rather a solitary soul and preferred a quiet life. Bébé refused to be convinced.

"That's what shy people always say," she told him with an air of complete authority. "But what they really mean is that they're afraid people won't like them and they don't want to risk a snub. But that wouldn't happen to *you*, Mr. Ravenscroft. Honestly, it wouldn't.

Particularly if—" she stopped short and smiled deprecatingly.

"Particularly if people deduce that you found my company desirable?" Charles finished, half amused, half annoyed by her complaisant belief in her own powers.

"Well, I wouldn't have put it just like that," Bébé said demurely. "But I *would* like us to be friends. You see, you're so *interest*ing. Not like these boys who haven't *done* anything with their lives and simply haven't anything *real* about them." She made a little gesture with her hands which dismissed to oblivion all the Tommys and Dickies and Joes who had worked so hard to win her approbation. "Oh, they're darlings, of course, but so *boring*!" and regarded Charles through her dark lashes to see how he took that.

And Charles, though he knew just how much that meant, found himself genuinely amused.

"You're flattering me," he declared gravely. "I'm afraid that in a very little while, you'll discover just how little I deserve your good opinion."

And Bébé, with an impudent grin, took the wind finally out of his sails by saying cheerfully :

"Oh, if that happens, you'll soon know! As soon as anybody bores me, I drop them like a—like a hot potato!"

"Ruthless but eminently practical," Charles commented. "Very well, on those terms, perhaps we could be friends." And he held out his hand as if to seal the bargain. "Always assuming, of course, that I have the same privileges," he added softly.

Bébé, her hand held firmly in his, gave a little gasp. She wasn't used to being treated in this off-hand manner, and besides, there was a challenging gleam in Charles's eyes which should have warned her. Instead, it simply acted as a spur.

"But of course!" she replied, wide-eyed with surprise that he could imagine anything else to be the case. "That's only fair. But I hope you won't want to ditch me because—" she paused as if to lay emphasis on what was coming—"I think we may find we've quite a lot in common—Charles!"

And with a flippant little salute, she left him to wonder just what he had let himself in for—and exactly what had been the significance of that last remark.

But almost immediately he shrugged away any feeling of misgiving. In fact, the more he contemplated it, the greater became the appeal of playing with fire. Bébé was, he fully recognised, both a shrewd and unscrupulous young woman, but not for a moment did he believe, despite her brazen pursuit of him, that her heart was in any way involved where he was concerned. No, she'd got something far more subtle than that in mind. She meant to make use of him in some way and it might be amusing to find out just what it was—and to pit his brains against hers in doing so.

The truth of it was that Alpenglühen had lost much of the appeal that it had had for him. It was easy enough to find an explanation for that, of course. He hadn't enough to do. That hadn't mattered at first. In fact, it had been just what he needed after all the stresses and strains he had experienced in the last few years. And if he wanted proof that to relax in circumstances which made no demands on him had been the right medicine, here it was. He felt fighting fit again and he wanted to be back in harness.

Not for the first time he considered the possibility of leaving Alpenglühen before his holiday was up, but one consideration in particular made him dismiss the idea. He had got to make the very utmost of this break because, once he got back to the hospital and took up his new post, heaven knew when he would be able to take another holiday of such long duration.

But even with his mind made up, he knew that to stay on would only be tolerable if some sort of diversion was available. Crossing swords with Bébé might well provide that.

With anyone as forthright as Bébé, the new alliance was bound to be quickly noticed and remarked on, sometimes with amusement, sometimes with surprise. In Nicky's case, with both.

"So it would seem that our superior Mr. Ravenscroft isn't entirely devoid of ordinary human weaknesses," he commented gleefully to Dinah. "Well, it should be an entertaining spectacle, to say the least of it! Rather like watching a circus elephant that's been taught to dance. Still, no doubt he'll enjoy himself—while it lasts. Because of course it won't. He's not Bébé's type—he'll bore her in no time, you'll see! In fact, for the life of me, I can't see why she's bothering herself to string him along at all. It can't be very amusing for her to spend so much time with a stuffed shirt like Ravenscroft!"

Dinah didn't reply. She was convinced that Bébé had found Nicky very attractive indeed—and small wonder, of course! What was more, she had made no attempt to hide her feelings. Consequently, the announcement of Nicky's engagement to another girl had come as a very real blow. But she wasn't going to let anyone else know that, and how better could she hide her injured pride than by gaily transferring all her interest to another man?

Being herself a woman, Dinah felt she could understand what was in Bébé's mind—even sympathise with it up to a point. But she couldn't help feeling that Charles wasn't being treated fairly. She didn't agree with Nicky that he was a stuffed shirt, but nor did she think that he was the sort of man to indulge in a meaningless flirtation. In fact, though she couldn't have said how she had come to such a conclusion, she was sure that to Charles, falling in love would be a very serious matter. And so, if Nicky was right in thinking that Bébé was simply amusing herself—or if Dinah's own interpretation of the situation was correct, then there was a very real possibility of Charles being badly hurt. And oddly enough, despite her original antagonism towards him, Dinah didn't welcome such a state of affairs.

"Hey!" Nicky challenged laughingly. "A penny for them!" and gave Dinah's hand a gentle shake,

With a little start she collected her wits. She couldn't possibly tell Nicky what was in her mind for she knew he'd never be able to understand—how could he when she didn't really understand herself? So it had got to be one of those hateful half-truths again.

"I was thinking about what you'd just said and wondering—Nicky, have you any idea how long the Vallaises are staying? And, for that matter, Mr. Ravenscroft?"

"I don't know about the Vallaises," Nicky admitted. "Nor for sure about Ravenscroft, though I'm under the impression that he won't be here much longer. Why?"

"Well, I think you're right—about Mr. Ravenscroft," Dinah said thoughtfully. "So, in that case—"

"Well?" Nicky asked impatiently as she paused.

"Only—it's not very long for anything very—very dramatic to happen, is it?" she amplified rather uncertainly.

"You mean, it doesn't give Bébé very much time to beguile him into submission?" Nicky suggested with a faint smile. "Oh, but darling, that's a process that needn't take any time at all! You should know that!"

"I should?" Dinah exclaimed in sudden panic. "Why do you say that, Nicky?"

"Why, darling, you're as white as a sheet!" Nicky said anxiously. "I only meant that it didn't take long for us to find out how we felt about one another."

"Oh!" Dinah relaxed, but the colour didn't return immediately to her cheeks. "How silly of me! I'm sorry, Nicky."

"Just what did you think I meant, Dinah?" he asked curiously.

She made a little groping movement with her hands. "I don't quite know," she admitted. "It was you speaking of being *beguiled into submission*. I'd simply hate to think—it—it sounds so degrading."

"I quite agree," Nicky said harshly, and changed the subject with such determination that Dinah knew they would never speak of it again.

With the constant coming and going of visitors, it wasn't always possible for Nicky to find another three

93

men with whom to play bridge—he made it a hard and fast rule never to play with women. His enforced inactivity didn't seem, however, to worry him, and Dinah rejoiced that he could devote his evenings to her.

But that state of affairs didn't last very long, for Mr. Vallaise announced wistfully one evening that being on holiday always made him feel that his brain was atrophying and that he'd give anything for a good evening of bridge. There was a little silence during which all the other men present looked at Nicky. But he made no effort to volunteer. Indeed, it wasn't until two other men had accepted the challenge that one of them said rather dryly:

"How about you, Gisborne? Or have you given up gambling since—" his eyes slid meaningly in Dinah's direction.

Nicky coloured at the suggestion that he was under a woman's thumb, but there was no hint of annoyance in his reply.

"I'll play—if you can't find anyone else to make up your four," he said easily. "But it will have to be on one condition. I've got a job to hold down. I had a heavy day today and I anticipate another one tomorrow. That being so, I want to turn in at a reasonable hour. Are you agreeable to setting an approximate time limit?"

The other three agreed without argument, though Mr. Vallaise regarded Nicky with a quizzically thoughtful expression which suggested that he was wondering whether there might not actually be some other reason for the condition. The look intensified when, having cut for partners, he and Nicky were in opposition to one another. It rather suggested that this was the way he had hoped things would turn out, and when play began, it wasn't difficult to understand why. Mr. Vallaise had been perfectly sincere when he had said he wanted to exercise his brain and having heard something of Nicky's reputation, had hoped for an opponent worthy of his steel.

And as the play progressed, he realised contentedly that he had found just that. So did Nicky. He quickly discovered that good though he knew himself to be, he had got to exert every ounce of concentration and ability he possessed if he didn't want to go down to this brilliant, poker-faced performer who seemed not only to have second sight, but also the ability to stir his less able partner to prodigious efforts.

Nicky drew a deep breath. He was pretty certain that, financially, he wouldn't benefit as much as he could usually expect to do. He might even be out of pocket, but for once money didn't matter. The sheer exhilaration of pitting his wits against such an opponent possessed him, and then even that vanished. He was conscious of no emotion whatever. He was an automaton, controlled by an ice-cold brain.

A man came past the table, halted and remained. He beckoned a friend and after that, curiosity brought others, including Charles. Apart from the players when they made their bids, no one spoke. Even Bébé, watching her father's intent face, was silent, and if anyone had had the time or interest to notice, there was an unusual tenseness about her as if what was going on was, to her, something far more important than a game of cards. For Dinah, too, there was tension. Even on other occasions when she had watched him play, she had never before seen this Nicky—utterly absorbed, entirely oblivious to everything except the cards he held and those that the other men played. A stranger to her.

"If I were to speak to him, he wouldn't hear," she thought with conviction, and she was afraid, not for herself, but for Nicky. Her own ability at card games was insignificant, but she knew enough to appreciate that she was watching masters at the game and that, for the time being, Nicky was completely under the spell of it. She had known before that he really enjoyed playing, but this utter absorption went beyond mere enjoyment. It was as if he was possessed by—by what? She didn't know, and that in itself was frightening.

The tension mounted as the fortunes of the game favoured first one pair and then the other. Mr. Vallaise and his partner won the first rubber, thanks to a brilliant finesse in the final game. Nicky and his partner won the second, but almost to the last minute, the result hung in the balance.

As the cards were being shuffled for the first game of the decisive rubber, Mr. Vallaise addressed Nicky directly.

"Care to double the stakes?" he asked placidly.

Nicky's eyes narrowed speculatively. Just what did that mean? Not over-confidence, he was sure. They were too well matched and Mr. Vallaise was far too experienced not to know that unguarded optimism can rob even the best player of victory. Gamesmanship, then? Again Nicky rejected the idea. If he was beaten, it would be by a man who, quite simply, played a better game than he did. There could be no question that such a man would stoop to attempt to undermine his opponent's confidence by, in effect, saying: "*You haven't got a chance*!" So there must be another reason, and he thought he knew what it was.

"I'd prefer to leave that decision to my partner," he said quietly, and looked across at him. "How do you feel about it?"

"I'm on," the other man replied laconically.

Mr. Vallaise smiled faintly and looked a query at his own partner.

"Yes," came the answer, even more briefly.

There was a longer pause than usual when the cards had been dealt and the four men studied their cards. Then play began. Nicky and his partner won the first game, Mr. Vallaise and his the second. Now everything depended on the third game, and the tension which had seemed already to have reached the limit, became positively painful as the bidding went the rounds. It was Nicky's call which finally went through, though only due to what seemed must be downright reckless-ness on his part, and when his partner's very mediocre hand was laid down, quite a few onlookers decided that the result was a foregone conclusion. Nicky, they were convinced, had overcalled his hand and couldn't hope to fulfil his contract.

But if Nicky shared their opinion, he showed no sign of it. He played with unhurried coolness, gained a trick here, lost one there with complete imperturbability until the point came in the game where he needed only one more trick to win. And then, for the first time, as two cards already lay on the table, he hesitated. Hesitated so long that it seemed as if his nerve had suddenly deserted him.

Nicky, if he had had time to think of anything of that sort, would have been amused. He knew perfectly well that he held the master card which would give him victory, but was that what he really wanted? Wasn't it possible that to lose might, in the end, bring far more lasting advantages than to beat a man who, clearly, was not used to losing? It could be—

The onlookers held their breath as the seconds ticked by and still he made no move. Unseen by anyone, Bébé crossed her fingers. Then, slowly, deliberately, Nicky played his card and finally, Mr. Vallaise played his— and the vital trick was Nicky's. But no more. He had only just achieved his objective.

Mr. Vallaise's hand shot across the table to seize Nicky's.

"I've never in all my life found losing so enjoyable!" he declared enthusiastically. "I'm reckoned to be pretty good, but you're my master, young man!"

For the first time since play had begun, Nicky smiled. So he had assessed his opponent correctly—he was big enough a man to accept defeat without resentment— big enough, too, to give ungrudging praise to his vanquisher.

"I've never had to work so hard to win!" he declared fervently. "And I must admit, I feel an absolute rag now. But I wouldn't have missed it for the world!"

Mr. Vallaise nodded understandingly.

"What you want is a pick-me-up," he declared, snapping his fingers to attract the attention of a waiter. "So do we all, come to that!"

And Nicky, who seemed entirely to have forgotten his earlier determination to go to bed early, agreed that that *was* just what he wanted. More chairs were pulled up round the card table so that Bébé and her mother could share in the celebrations. Dinah, too, was included, and so, to his vexation, was Charles. He wasn't a heavy-drinking man and he could see this party going on indefinitely. Oh well, no doubt he would be able to make his escape reasonably soon—which was more than Dinah would have a chance of doing, he thought with a feeling of compassion. She would have to stick it out because, if she didn't, young Gisborne wouldn't like it. He wanted her here, the self-satisfied young ass, as part of his admiring audience.

In which Charles was less than fair to him. Nicky had not exaggerated when he had said that he felt like a rag. He had played himself completely out, and for the time being, it was beyond his ability to make even the most simple decision. He had very little to say for himself and Mr. Vallaise appeared to be in like case, though he was frowning faintly as if something puzzled him. In fact, the celebration would have fallen rather flat if Bébé hadn't taken matters into her hands and infused at least some gaiety into the proceedings. But it was actually Mrs. Vallaise who galvanised them all into sudden awareness.

"You know, Mr. Gisborne, I just don't understand you English!" she declared aggressively during a little lull in the conversation.

Nicky looked at her thoughtfully. He had no liking for Mrs. Vallaise whom he regarded as being both self-opinionated and despotic. But tonight he felt that he could be tolerant, even to her. On the other hand, he had no intention of lying down under an unprovoked attack.

"I'm sorry about that, Mrs. Vallaise," he said cheerfully. "Is there anything that I can explain? Just what do you find wrong with us?"

"Your lack of enterprise," snapped the lady robustly. "No initiative at all, that's what!"

"Now, Momma," Mr. Vallaise said placatingly. "We're all friends here, I'm sure. We don't want—"

"Oh, but I'd like to hear more," Nicky insisted, his voice dangerously soft. "I'm very much interested!"

"So you should be," Mrs. Vallaise told him belligerently. "It was you I had in mind!"

Dinah caught her breath. Just why Mrs. Vallaise should attack Nicky like this she had no idea, but it was unpleasant to say the least of it, and it would be expecting too much of him to tolerate such downright rudeness without protest. Unconsciously she laid her hand on Nicky's arm, silently imploring him not to make a difficult situation still worse. But Nicky seemed to take the gesture as encouragement, for he sat up very upright in his chair and faced his tormenter unflinchingly.

Bébé and her father exchanged glances. There was a question in her eyes, but very slightly, Mr. Vallaise shook his head. Evidently he felt that the situation was beyond him—or was it that, in some way, he thought his wife's indiscretion could be turned to his own advantage? Charles, who had noticed the byplay, wasn't too sure.

"So I supposed," Nicky drawled coolly. "And no doubt you're entitled to your opinion. But I would like to know on just what you base it, Mrs. Vallaise."

"Isn't it obvious? Here are you, a young, strong man with an exceptionally good brain! Oh, I admit that! You wouldn't have got the better of my husband if it weren't so. Yet you make no use of it to get on in the world. Now that's a shameful state of affairs, I consider, and one which I just can't understand."

"I see your point," Nicky admitted blandly. "And I grant you, my present job isn't a very remunerative one. But—" he shrugged his shoulders fatalistically—"if opportunity doesn't come one's way—"

"You think opportunity should come to you—not that you should make it for yourself?" Mr. Vallaise asked with interest.

Nicky turned to him quickly.

"I think opportunity is more often the result of being the right man in the right place at the right time than anything else," he said thoughtfully. "Naturally, one has to be able to recognise it when it comes, and be ready to make the most of it. But that's a different matter from

99

being a ruthless go-getter. Of course, that's only my opinion, but personally—" he grinned disarmingly. "If I were a boss, I wouldn't be too keen on employing excessively ambitious young men who had a permanent eye on the main chance! I'd be too scared that they'd be ousting me from my own job next!"

Mr. Vallaise chuckled appreciatively.

"Something in that," he admitted. "Eh, Momma?"

Mrs. Vallaise shrugged her shoulders.

"It's an opinion, no doubt," she remarked indifferently as if she had entirely lost interest in the topic. But not in her determination to control events. She stood up, as small and slight a figure as her own daughter yet with an even greater air of unshakeable belief in her own supreme rightness than Bébé had. "Come, Henry, it's long past your bedtime," she announced with bland authority. "You know how it upsets you if you don't have a good eight hours' sleep!"

"Oh, once in a way doesn't do any harm," Mr. Vallaise protested, though without much hope.

"That's how all bad habits start," Mrs. Vallaise told him austerely. "Anyway, you've already had more than enough to drink for one evening!" And picking up her handbag, she turned from the table with an air of finality which brooked no further argument.

With a resigned shrug, Mr. Vallaise accepted the inevitable, though he still had sufficient spirit left to pause for a final word with Nicky.

"Thank you for a most enjoyable evening, Gisborne," he said pleasantly, and held out his hand.

Instantly Nicky jumped to his feet.

"It was good, wasn't it?" he said with boyish enthusiasm as they shook hands. "I'd like to repeat it some time, if you're agreeable?"

"Yes, indeed," Mr. Vallaise agreed cordially. He paused momentarily and then went on deliberately: "I'd also like, some time when we're on our own, to hear more about your ideas on opportunity!" He chuckled reminiscently. "They interest me considerably!"

"I'd like that," Nicky declared, suddenly serious.

Mr. Vallaise nodded and turned to follow his wife. As he did so, Bébé slipped her arm through his and with a gay wave of her hand, left the rest of the party to its own devices.

It soon broke up until only Dinah and Nicky were left. Indeed Nicky, slumped in his chair, his hands deep in his pockets, his feet straight out before him, seemed completely oblivious to his surroundings. He was smiling faintly as if his thoughts were pleasant ones and when Dinah spoke, he started violently.

"Sorry, I was miles away!" he apologised. "Good lord, everybody else gone? Then I suppose we'd better follow suit." He stood up, yawned and stretched extravagantly. "Golly, what an evening!"

"You were wonderful!" Dinah said warmly. "I'm not much of a bridge player, but this evening I was absolutely fascinated!"

"Oh, that!" Nicky dismissed his victory with a careless shrug. "Yes, it was quite good fun. But it was what happened afterwards that was really important."

"Afterwards?" Dinah looked puzzled. "But nothing happened afterwards—except that Mrs. Vallaise was very rude to you!"

"Yes, wasn't she?" he agreed, chuckling. "Mad clean through because I'd beaten her old man! Well, bless her for it, I say. She didn't mean to, of course, but she gave me just the chance I'd been hoping for."

"The chance for what?" Dinah asked, still completely befogged.

Nicky put his hands on her shoulders and rocked her gently to and fro.

"The chance to catch the boss's eye good and proper," he explained gleefully. "Oh, maybe he'd got his eye on me in any case—certainly after I'd licked him, particularly as both he and I knew that I could have given him the game—if I hadn't decided that he wasn't the sort of man who would enjoy winning on those terms! He liked that, but what clinched it was that, thanks to Lady Macbeth, I had a marvellous opportunity of telling him my point of view about things that I'm pretty sure he feels are important." He smiled reminiscently. "That combined with the fact that, without unpleasantness, I rather cut the ground from under his lady wife's feet. Dinah—" his eyes were sparkling with excitement—"how would you like to live in America?"

"America?" she repeated, her mouth suddenly dry. "But—"

"Darling, don't you see?" There was more than a hint of impatience in the way Nicky spoke. "I'm willing to bet that within a matter of days, old man Vallaise will offer me a job—a *real* job!"

"And you'd take it?" Dinah asked.

"Take it?" he stared at her in blank amazement. "Of course I would!"

CHAPTER SIX

BUT as the days passed, Nicky admitted to Dinah that he had evidently been wrong about Mr. Vallaise's intentions, for, though he didn't avoid Nicky, he certainly didn't seek his company.

But despite his disappointment, Nicky seemed more puzzled than annoyed.

"I wonder why the old chap's hanging fire," he cogitated. "It's not in character. He's the sort that acts promptly, once he's made up his mind. I'm quite sure of that. And yet—" he shook his head—"something is making him hesitate."

"Or somebody?" Dinah suggested sympathetically. She might not like the idea of living in America, still less did she want Nicky to work for Mr. Vallaise, with all the resulting difficulties she felt could result from that, but least of all did she enjoy seeing Nicky disappointed of something on which he had set his heart. "Mrs. Vallaise?"

Nicky looked at her sharply.

"Mrs. Vallaise," he repeated thoughtfully. "No, on the whole, I don't think so. Oh, I know she's got a poor opinion of me and she's a lady who likes to have the last word, but my reading of the situation is that while the old man gives her an absolutely free hand—or she takes it—in domestic affairs, where business is concerned, he's his own man. Probably they both regard that as a fair division of labour—he makes the money, she spends it! No, I don't think she's the culprit. Nor, for that matter, is Bébé, and for the same reason. Fond though he is of her, it simply wouldn't occur to him to admit her into what he regards as exclusively a man's world. Oh, confound it, why aren't I a thought-reader!" And he rubbed his forehead vigorously as if to stimulate his mind to activity.

"There is just one thing—" Dinah said diffidently.

"What?" Nicky demanded.

"Well, don't you remember what Mrs. Vallaise said about him drinking—that he'd had all of enough for one evening," Dinah reminded him. "Suppose that was true, isn't it possible—" she hesitated, troubled by the morose expression that the suggestion had brought to Nicky's face.

"That he said more than he felt like standing by in the sober light of day?" he finished harshly. "Yes, I suppose it could be that. No, I'm hanged if I do. He didn't have a thing to drink during the whole time that we were playing and not very much after that. Besides, if ever I've met a man who knows his capacity to the ounce, Vallaise is that one! No, it's a mystery to me—and a confounded nuisance too, after all the spadework I put in. Oh well, there it is!" And he shrugged his shoulders in that fatalistic way which Dinah had noticed before. Nicky, she had felt for some time, was not the sort of person to waste his time in useless regret, no matter how disappointed he might be, and it seemed to her that this might be a good time to suggest an idea that had been in her mind for some time, though she had not had the courage to speak about it until now.

"Nicky—" she said diffidently.

"M'm?" For all that he had apparently dismissed his hopes he was evidently still thinking about them, for he sounded both abstracted and a little impatient at the interruption.

"Do you remember—" Dinah's eyes were downcast as she traced the outline of a pattern on the material of her dress. "You said something once about—an opportunity you'd like to take if only you'd got the money—"

"Did I?" Nicky said vaguely. "Oh yes, I remember. Well, what about it?"

"Only—I was wondering—you said it would be a goldmine," Dinah said breathlessly. "Couldn't we go into it as partners?"

"You mean—on your cash?" Nicky said with a lack of enthusiasm which made Dinah's heart sink.

"My money—your—your know-how," Dinah explained eagerly. "One would be no good without the other so—so it really would be a partnership, wouldn't it?"

Nicky shook his head.

"No go. It's too late. Another man has taken up the option."

"Oh, Nicky!" Dinah exclaimed in dismay. "If only I'd suggested it sooner—"

"No, that's nothing for you to fret about," Nicky assured her. "It's just as well you didn't do anything of the sort because, on second thoughts, I came to the conclusion that it wasn't such a good idea after all. In fact, you might well have lost your money. So don't give it another thought! Promise?"

"Yes, if you're quite sure, Nicky," Dinah said waveringly. "I mean, you're not just saying that so that I won't be upset?"

"Word of a scout," Nicky vowed. "So now forget all about it, there's a good girl!"

"All right," Dinah agreed. "But, Nicky, if something else does turn up that—that interests you, promise you'll let me know and—and be a partner."

"I promise," Nicky said abstractedly. "But in the meantime, will you do something else for me?"

"Of course I will, Nicky," Dinah said eagerly. "You know I'll do anything—"

A peculiar expression passed across Nicky's face and was gone.

"It's nothing to do with money," he explained. "Simply, I want you to remember that I don't want the Vallaise family—any one of them—to get the impression either that I'm over-anxious to get a job or that I'm disappointed because the old man hasn't come up to expectations. It wouldn't do any good and it might—" he stopped short and started again. "What I mean is that I can't bring myself to beg for favours. I know it sounds petty-minded," he concluded with a wry smile. "But failure though I am, I've still got some pride left!"

"You're not a failure," Dinah insisted firmly. "But

all the same, I think you're right. I mean, to me, it seems like *proper* pride—and I think there's something else that could be important."

"Yes?" Nicky said curiously.

"You said that Mr. Vallaise isn't the sort of man who would ever want to win for any other reason than his own skill."

"Well?" Nicky encouraged, his eyes narrowing slightly.

"Well," Dinah explained earnestly. "If that's so, then I think he must be what I'd call a *strong* man—and doesn't that mean that he wouldn't be inclined either to respect or trust a man who kow-towed to him and begged for favours?

Nicky was startled. What Dinah had just said was something he had been quick to appreciate. Mr. Vallaise *might* be deliberately putting him to the test to see how he reacted in such trying circumstances. Indeed, really it was that which had lain behind his request to Dinah. But he had never expected her to work out such a sophisticated conclusion all by herself. He had even been careful not to suggest it because he had felt that she might find it rather too unpleasantly calculating!

"I think you've got something there," he told her thoughtfully as if what she had said had come as an entirely new idea to him. He put his arm round her and hugged her close. "My precious little strategist, what would I do without you!"

"And next week." Bébé said gaily, "we'll go on one of those moonlight sleigh drives Frau Emil was talking about. They sound like heaven!"

"Sorry, but you must count me out," Charles replied briefly.

"But why?" Bébé demanded. "Don't be a spoilsport! It will be tremendous fun!"

Charles shook his head.

"I shan't be here," he explained. "My holiday ends before then."

"Oh, *Charles*!" Bébé's face crumpled like that of a

disappointed child. "But you can't go, you simply *can't*! Not when everything is working out so well."

Charles regarded her with considerable interest. He had never for a moment imagined that Bébé's unremitting pursuit of him was the outcome of anything even approaching love. What he had been sure of was that she meant to make use of him in some way, though he had not been able to discover just how. But the situation had intrigued him and he had permitted her to lead him by the nose so that he might find out just what this outrageous girl was up to. But she had kept her own counsel with amazing tenacity and he was no nearer to plumbing the depths of her mind than he had been to begin with. Now, for the first time, she had at least admitted that she had got some ploy on hand and that he was an integral part of it. It seemed likely that he might conceivably learn more.

"What's working out so well?" he asked, his eyes still on her downcast face. Her dark eyes met his and he saw doubt and indecision in them. She was obviously not sure if she could trust him.

"Well—" she said reluctantly—"if I tell you—will you stay on?"

"No, I won't," Charles said unequivocally. "I can't. I told you, my holiday is coming to an end and I must get back to my work."

"Your work," Bébé repeated slowly. "What *is* your work, Charles? Is it something you're ashamed of—because you've never given me, or anyone else so far as I can find out, the least hint of what you do."

"Don't sidetrack," Charles requested sternly. "And don't trouble to answer my question if you don't want to. I'm not all that interested." And he made as if to stand up.

"Don't be a beast, Charles," Bébé begged plaintively, putting a restraining hand on his arm. "I'll tell you—though I don't suppose you'll either understand or approve. Men usually get all put out with women's tactics. It's because they're so much more sentimental than we are."

"Really!" Charles said sceptically.

"Oh yes," Bébé assured him calmly. "We're far more practical than you are. We have to be!" She paused, frowning and nibbling her finger as if she didn't quite know what to say. Then she announced abruptly: "This engagement—it won't do, you know."

He knew very well to what engagement she was referring, but startled by the sudden introduction of the topic, he attempted to gain time.

"What engagement?"

Bébé's hands fluttered impatiently.

"Oh, don't pretend you don't know! Nicky's and Dinah's, of course."

Charles shrugged his shoulders.

"Whether, in your opinion, it will or it won't do, it's none of your business—or mine either, for that matter."

"Oh yes, it is," Bébé contradicted truculently. "When you see two people making complete idiots of themselves, you can't just stand on the sidelines and cheer! You have to—to—" she paused uncertainly.

"Save them from themselves?" Charles suggested ironically. "From purely disinterested motives, of course?"

Bébé grinned disarmingly.

"Not altogether," she admitted blandly. "I admit to having—a soft spot for Nicky myself, but though I don't expect you to believe it, I really like Dinah. She's nice—much nicer than I am!"

"You can say that again!" Charles told her, and was disconcerted to see something oddly like satisfaction gleam momentarily in Bébé's eyes.

"At least that's one thing we agree on," she replied coolly. "Can't you go one further and admit that you know perfectly well that they're just not suited? They don't add up!"

"I bow to your superior judgment," Charles said dryly, though to himself he admitted that he thought she was probably right.

"You see," Bébé went on reflectively, "their outlook on life is so different—they want such different things from it. Can't you feel that? Dinah's a bit older than I am, but all the same, she's still just a romantic kid. She hasn't got beyond the moonlight and roses stage. As for Nicky—" she paused, grimaced and shrugged her shoulders. "Well, anyone with their wits about them to the degree that you have can answer that! He's an adventurer, out for excitement—and money!"

"And that's the man you're in love with!" Charles commented caustically.

"Yes, but then I understand because I'm the same sort! Oh yes, I am. That's why I put excitement first and money second. He wants that all right, but he wants the thrill of getting it by—by his own endeavours and at some risk! Now, Dinah will never understand that, and it will hurt her. I think she's got quite a lot of money herself, you know, otherwise Nicky would never have got engaged to her even if she'd attracted him. But the point is, she'll hand it all to him on a plate —and that would soon bore Nicky. In fact," she concluded reflectively, "I'm pretty sure it's begun to already."

"I've seen no signs of it," Charles told her shortly.

"Oh well!" Bébé said compassionately. "After all, you're only a man even if you are more intelligent than most. But you can take my word for it—"

"All right," Charles agreed impatiently, "I'll take your word for that and for everything else you've said. I'll also admit that if you're determined to interfere then neither I nor anyone else will be able to stop you. But I defy you to produce one single reason which will hold water why I should involve myself!"

"Oh, for heaven's sake!" Bébé exclaimed in sheer exasperation. "Because you're in love with Dinah, of course!"

"I'm *what*?" Charles shouted.

"In love with Dinah," Bébé repeated calmly. "Oh yes, you are! You give yourself away time after time!"

"Do I, indeed!" Charles said grimly. "Perhaps you'll explain just how I do that."

"Well, for one thing, you're always watching her—"

"I watch you, too," said Charles. "And if you're under the delusion that on that account, I'm in love with you—"

"Oh, that!" Bébé dismissed the idea with an airy wave of the hand. "You watch me because you never know what I'll be up to next and you find that amusing. But with Dinah—that's something quite different."

"Is that so?" Charles ejaculated, momentarily nonplussed by Bébé's complaisant air of infallibility.

"Of course it is. We're totally different types, Dinah and I. I'm a mixture of Poppa's shrewdness and Momma's bossiness. At present I get away with it because I'm young and pretty, but when I get older, I shall be a holy terror. Unless, of course, I happen to marry someone who prefers to be boss himself—which could be quite exciting," she reflected pensively. "But never mind me. It's Dinah we're talking about. Now, she's sweet and warmhearted. All the same, she's got plenty of spunk, so there's nothing too sugary about her. But there's something else as well." She frowned and went on slowly as if she was choosing her words with care. "I know what it is, though I don't understand why it should be, but she's *vulnerable*—far more so than most people are. Yes, I know, you're surprised that I, of all people, should have seen that. But you've seen it as well, and that's why you're always on the watch—in case she needs a helping hand. Now, aren't I right?"

"You're quite right, she is vulnerable," Charles agreed. "And I admit to a certain concern for her on that account. But that doesn't mean—"

"Oh yes, it does," Bébé contradicted firmly. "When a man like you feels all protective about a particular girl it *always* means he's in love with her. So what I want to know is—what are you going to do about it?"

"Nothing," Charles declared curtly. "For one thing, you're basing your conclusions on a completely false premise. And for another, there's absolutely nothing that I can do about it."

"Now, that's where I don't agree with you," Bébé drawled coolly. "So just you listen!"

Charles listened with growing revulsion and incredulity. When at last she had said her say and was waiting expectantly for his reply, he didn't spare her.

"You rapacious young harpy" he exclaimed disgustedly. "I'll have nothing whatever to do with such arrant double-dealing"

"Why ever not?" Bébé asked in surprise. "It's quite practical—and you know what they say about all's fair—"

"Be quiet," Charles ordered and, with a shrug, Bébé complied. After all, men always took rather a long time digesting a new idea—

"Look here, I can't have got it right," Charles said despairingly at last. "You simply can't mean that, with your father's help, you're going to put pressure on Gisborne so that it would be to his advantage to jilt Dinah?"

"And to her advantage as well," Bébé said softly. "Don't forget that"

Charles, however, took no notice.

"But just in case Gisborne should have any remnants of decency in his make-up, you want to be able to convince him that really he's got nothing to worry about because Dinah is in love with me? Right, so far?"

"Absolutely," Bébé approved. "I said you were intelligent, Charles."

"And in order to add verisimilitude to an extremely unconvincing story, I've got to drop you and show signs of being in love with Dinah so that, when Gisborne defaults, it will save her pride to have another man to turn to. In other words, I'm to catch her on the rebound."

"That's it," Bébé acknowledged with shameless pride. "It's a real lollapaloosa—it simply couldn't fail."

"I don't care a damn whether it would work or not," Charles told her icily. "It's an utterly despicable idea—do you honestly imagine that any man—" he stopped and shook his head. "No, it's no good trying to make you see that. You simply haven't got the ability to understand the meaning of common decency." He stood up with an air of finality. "But there are one or two things you've *got* to understand. To begin with, I'm not going to play your game even for the few days that I shall be here. And nor is anybody or anything going to persuade me to extend my holiday. Is that clear?"

Bébé lay back in her armchair, completely relaxed and entirely unperturbed.

"You should cross your fingers when you say that," she drawled tauntingly. "It's tempting the fates to be so positive, you know."

Charles gave up. She would never understand if he argued for a month of Sundays. He terminated the conversation by turning his back on her and walking towards the door.

But even then, Bébé didn't give up.

"You know, Charles, I really don't understand you!" she announced wonderingly.

"I know you don't," he acknowledged without turning. "You haven't got the necessary mental equipment to be able to."

"Maybe that's so," she concluded. "But I wasn't thinking about me. I was thinking about *you*. You see, though I don't know much about you, I know one thing for sure. You're an ambitious man, Charles, and in your own way, quite as ruthless as I am—or as Nicky is. Oh yes, you are. It sticks out a mile. I bet, in your time, you've pushed quite a few folk aside if they got in your way. Now, isn't that so?"

Charles made no reply, but for an appreciable time he stood stock still, his hand on the doorknob. Then he went out of the room and shut the door quietly behind him.

"Well, for goodness' sake!" Bébé gasped, bright-eyed and alert. "I certainly put my finger on something that time! But just what, I wonder?"

"That's odd," Nicky remarked.

"What is?" Dinah asked, since she hadn't noticed anything happening which was at all out of the way.

"Why, Ravenscroft's just come in and though Bébé's in her usual place and he must have seen her, he's gone right past her to the other end of the bar without so much as a glance in her direction!"

Dinah saw that he was right and saw, too, that

Charles's face was set in grim, forbidding lines which clearly indicated that something was wrong. Bébé, too, was not her usual gay self. She looked depressed, even miserable.

"Had a row," Nicky diagnosed.

"Well, you did say that you didn't think their— friendship would last," Dinah reminded him.

"I know I did," Nicky acknowledged. "But I'd taken it for granted that she'd be the one to make the break, whereas obviously it's the other way round."

Dinah gave another quick glance at the two faces.

"Do you think so?" she said dubiously. "Mr. Ravenscroft looks very much annoyed—"

"He certainly does." Nicky didn't sound in the least regretful. "But it's Bébé I'm going by. If she'd given Ravenscroft the brush-off, it wouldn't worry her in the least. Instead of which, she looks as miserable as a wet hen, poor kid!"

Dinah, remembering how thankful Nicky had been when Bébé had transferred her interest from himself to Charles, was surprised by his final words.

"But I thought you didn't like her," she exclaimed, and instantly saw from Nicky's expression that she had said the wrong thing. None the less, his reply gave no indication that she had vexed him.

"Oh, she's spoilt and a bit of a scatterbrain," he said tolerantly. "But actually, she's not a bad kid."

Dinah didn't reply. In fact, she could think of nothing to say, for she felt suddenly chilled. Though he had made no further reference to his hope that Mr. Vallaise would offer him a job, Dinah felt sure that he hadn't really dismissed the idea and in his determination to keep on the right side of the family, he could even forget his earlier dislike of Bébé. Instantly she reproached herself for ascribing such cynical expediency to Nicky, but at that moment, he spoke again.

"She's going," he announced. "Let's ask her to have a drink with us, shall we?"

And without waiting for Dinah's answer, he got up and intercepted Bébé before she reached the door. Evidently it took several moments to persuade Bébé.

Then Nicky went to the bar and Bébé came slowly over to join Dinah.

"Nicky says you want me to have a drink with you," she said dubiously. "Are you really sure you do?"

Dinah would have given a lot to have been able to reply with a blunt : "No, I don't!" but that, of course, was out of the question, and besides, Bébé did look unhappy.

"Of course we do," she insisted with a show of cordiality which apparently satisfied Bébé, for without further ado, she sat down, though the smile she gave Dinah was rather watery.

"I'm afraid I won't be very good company," she said with a little sigh. "I've got a bad attack of the mulli-grubs."

"Oh—well, I suppose we all get that way some-times," Dinah said encouragingly. "We—we must try to cheer you up."

Bébé gave her a quick look which seemed to hold both gratitude and, rather surprisingly perhaps, a hint of shame.

"You're nice," she said impulsively. "Much nicer than I am!"

Fortunately for Dinah, she was spared the necessity of replying to such an embarrassing remark by Nicky's return with the drinks.

For a moment or so there was rather a difficult silence. Then all three of them broke it at the same instant, only to become silent again with equal simul-taneousness. And in the confusion and laughter which followed, the ice was broken. Conversation admittedly wasn't very brilliant, but after a while Bébé did seem to cheer up and played her part. Nor did she make any attempt to monopolise Nicky. Indeed, the topics which she introduced were so very much of entirely feminine interest that Nicky was rather left out of it. After a time, not unnaturally, he grew a little bored and cut across with a remark about the skiing prospects in the next few days.

"Not too good, it appears," he said ruefully. "Emil says there's a warning been put out of snow on the way and he seems to have taken it pretty seriously. He's posted up a notice on the board that simply bristles with 'Achtungs' in huge red letters!"

"Oh well, perhaps it won't last long," Bébé said hopefully.

Nicky laughed.

"What you mean is that since it would interfere with your highness's pleasure, it had better *not* last!"

"I think other people might find it even more of a nuisance than I would," Bébé said thoughtfully. "I mean, if it's really bad, I suppose it could mean that all the planes would be grounded and people would be stuck here!" And her eyes slid in Charles's direction.

Dinah had seen the look and involuntarily she glanced in the same direction—only to find her eyes held in a fascination that held not a little fear. For Charles met her eyes steadily and she knew that he was trying to tell her something. She forced herself to look away, but not before she had read his message. He was warning her of something—something unpleasant, for there was also more than a hint of that humiliating pity which had so angered her on a previous occasion.

She took little part in the conversation after that, but when Nicky asked if there was anything wrong, she managed to laugh and say lightly that she thought the mulligrubs must be catching, for Bébé had evidently passed them on to her.

"Oh, I do hope not." Bébé exclaimed with every sign of distress. "Never mind, I'm going now, so you'll be able to enjoy your tête-à-tête without me here to spoil it." And with a wistful little smile, she got up and left them.

"Well, you might have made her a bit more welcome after what I told you about keeping in—" Nicky complained sulkily. "You positively froze her out!"

But Dinah hardly heard him. She had the unwelcome feeling that if she would only allow herself to admit it, she might perhaps understand Charles's warning.

Nicky and Bébé—no, she wouldn't let herself believe it. To do so would be disloyal to Nicky and that was unthinkable. So it must be that Charles was simply trying to make mischief and the fact that he might be feeling jealous because Bébé had so soon tired of his companionship was no excuse at all.

Well, thank goodness, he'd be leaving in a few days. Or would he, if that warning of bad weather was correct?

The forecast was correct. The snow began to fall heavily, relentlessly, silently. And it was the silence which was least easy to tolerate. It suggested that this was an effortless performance on the part of nature, one which could be kept up indefinitely. And after two days and nights without cessation, it began to seem as if nothing could stop it.

The first day hadn't been so bad. Being confined to the hotel was a nuisance, of course, but one could read or play cards or catch up with neglected correspondence. There was a gramophone and plenty of modern dance records and the younger visitors rolled back the rugs in the foyer and danced whenever the mood seized them. There was a rather more formal dance in the evening, too, and bedtime found everyone quite cheerful. It was still snowing heavily, but it would surely have stopped by morning.

But it hadn't. As persistently as ever, the bland white flakes fluttered down. A thick white blanket covered the steeply sloping roof of the hotel. Trees bowed under the weight they had never been meant to bear and paths that had been laboriously cleared the previous day had to be cleared once again, only to be smothered almost at once.

The Bergers were considerably worried, though they did their best not to show it, giving cheerful assurances that food and drink and fuel supplies were more than adequate. But there was one question which they couldn't answer :

"When will it stop?"

No one could answer that. Such a heavy fall so late in the season was unusual and consequently unpredictable. But looking at the sky, ominous with heavy, pregnant cloud, few people had any doubts what the answer would be—"*Not yet!*" And that was borne out by the weather forecasts.

Boredom was the chief enemy at first. Then came the feeling of imprisonment. The Bergers, backed by a few of the more experienced visitors, did their best to provide entertainment. Competitions were arranged, anyone who had any sort of talent was pressed into service and if the resulting concert was rather painfully amateurish, it served to pass the time.

But that was just it. There was so much time and after all, having planned an out-of-door holiday, who wanted to spend it cooped up in an hotel, however comfortable.

Nerves began to fray—Nicky's among them. In fact, to Dinah he was among the worst affected, and that was understandable enough since, as he pointed out, though for the rest of them it admittedly meant a spoilt holiday, for him it meant loss of work and consequently of pay.

"Much more of this and I shall be on my beam ends," he remarked moodily, staring out at the remorseless snow. "Just my confounded luck! And with old man Vallaise insisting on me making up his four, I don't even stand a chance of making a bit at cards. Oh, confound it! When will it stop?"

Dinah tried to think of something consoling to say, but without success. She wasn't feeling at all happy herself, partly because Nicky was so moody and partly because, owing to the amount of bridge that the two men were playing together, she and Nicky had somehow been drawn into the Vallaise family circle and there seemed to be no escape from it. Dinah found it particularly trying because it was very difficult to be friendly. Mrs. Vallaise observed none of the restraint usual between mere acquaintances. If she wanted to know anything, she asked for information with a directness that made it extremely difficult to avoid telling her far more than one wished to without telling a downright lie, since the other possibility—telling her to mind her own business—was out of the question. Nor did Bébé's attempts to persuade her mother to be more

117

circumspect do any good. Indeed, it sometimes seemed that they only made matters worse. On one occasion when, laughingly, she had told her mother that she really must let Dinah keep some of her secrets to herself, Mrs. Vallaise had reacted instantly and typically.

"I don't like secretiveness," she announced impressively. "Particularly in a young girl! It suggests that she's got something to hide—something not to her credit!"

After that, Dinah did the only thing left to her. She avoided Mrs. Vallaise whenever possible, though that meant spending much of her time in her own room since all the public rooms were fully occupied and Mrs. Vallaise might be in any one of them. However, an hour before dinner, the lounge was deserted in favour of the bar, and with a little sigh of relief, Dinah settled herself in one of the comfortable armchairs and closed her eyes. But she wasn't left in undisputed possession for long.

"Hallo, something wrong?" Nicky's voice asked uncertainly.

"Yes," Dinah told him flatly without opening her eyes. "There is! I'm quite, quite tired of being cross-questioned by an ill-bred, inquisitive woman who would be the first to resent anyone quizzing her!"

"If you mean Mrs. Vallaise—" Nicky began.

Dinah's eyes opened and she sat up abruptly.

"Yes, I do mean Mrs. Vallaise," she admitted bluntly. "And I'm sorry, Nicky, but even if it upsets you, I can't pretend to be friendly any more. It's just not possible."

"Oh, it's only her way of showing interest—" Nicky replied uneasily.

"Interest!" Dinah repeated hotly. "Do you know what she's interested in? In how much money I've got and whether I'm free to do what I like with it. Whether you've got any other means than what you earn. When we're going to get married and—you can believe it or not—whether you intend to work, once we're married."

Nicky flushed dully.

"Impertinent old harridan," he said wrathfully. And then, anxiously: "You didn't upset her, did you?"

118

Dinah closed her eyes again in a vain attempt to keep back the tears.

"I expect I did," she said wearily. "I told her as little as possible as politely as I could, but of course she drew the worst conclusions from that. She thinks I've got something I'm ashamed of to hide. So I've avoided her and I intend to go on doing that, Nicky. So please don't try to persuade me not to because it won't be any good!"

"You're not being very helpful, are you?" Nicky complained. "Don't you realise how important it is that you should make a good impression in that quarter? I mean—"

"I know what you mean," Dinah interrupted in a hard voice. "You mean that a man, however brilliant he may be, could be turned down if his wife—or in this case, his fiancée—is regarded as socially inadequate?"

"Well, yes," Nicky admitted awkwardly, and plunged on earnestly, "After all, it makes sense, Dinah. A wife who doesn't or can't back her husband is—well—"

"A liability," Dinah said bitterly. "In that case, Nicky, there seems to be only one way out." And she pulled off the ring she had worn for so short a time and held it out to him.

Instantly Nicky was all contrition. Of course he hadn't meant that! The last thing he wanted was for their engagement to be broken. He was sorry if he had upset her, but—for the first time in his life, his nerves were on edge.

"And so are yours, darling," he insisted soothingly. "It's this confounded snow. We're all at too close quarters for comfort, but once we can get out again, everything will be all right, I promise you."

She listened and let herself be convinced because she wanted to be and because she felt too tired to fight any more.

"All right, Nicky, I'll do my best," she promised wearily at length. "But honestly, I can't take any more just yet. You'd better say that I've got a bad headache—it's quite true, I have—and I shall probably go to bed quite soon."

"Well, perhaps it would be best," Nicky agreed. "Best for you, I mean. I'll say you just want to be quiet—"

"Yes, say that," Dinah agreed, and closed her eyes again.

For a moment he hesitated. Then she heard him go out of the room.

She leaned back against the soft cushions, thankful not to need to do anything but relax—if she could. Her head was throbbing painfully, but that wasn't the worst pain. That came from the knowledge that she and Nicky had practically quarrelled and so nearly parted. That hurt intolerably—and frighteningly.

But quietness and solitude began to play their part and she surrendered to the blissful drowsiness that possessed her.

Suddenly she was wide awake, aroused by someone making a sound so slight that it suggested extreme caution.

She looked in the direction of the sound and saw that a man was tiptoeing out of the writing room which opened off the lounge.

It was Charles Ravenscroft.

CHAPTER SEVEN

DINAH jumped to her feet and confronted Charles, her hands clenched.

"You were listening !" she accused.

"Unfortunately, yes," he admitted distastefully.

Dinah flushed, but she held her ground.

"You could have let us know that you were in there !"

"Naturally, I thought of that," Charles replied. "But there didn't seem to be any point in your conversation when I could emerge without causing embarrassment all round. So I decided to keep quiet in the hope that I could escape later undetected—as I almost did," he concluded regretfully.

If Dinah had stopped to think, she might have believed him, but in her present tense, troubled state of mind it was all too easy to look for a scapegoat on whom to blame everything, and she had found him in Charles.

"And now," she stormed, "I suppose you're going to make more mischief by telling everybody that Nicky and I—" she bit her lip, unable, even though Charles had heard everything, to admit that she and Nicky had quarrelled.

But Charles didn't seem to notice her concluding words. Instead, he repeated sharply :

"*More* mischief ?"

"Yes, *more* mischief," Dinah plunged on recklessly. "Oh, don't try to deny it. Right from the very first— over Nicky being so good at cards—"

He looked at her curiously.

"That episode, I should have thought, is better forgotten," he announced judicially. "Certainly I should imagine Gisborne would prefer it that way."

"Oh? Why?" Dinah demanded suspiciously.

"Because, by being so pugnacious, he made me, and other people present, wonder whether there might not be something in the idea that he owed his success to something more than skill and good luck," Charles told her bluntly.

"But you *know* he doesn't cheat," Dinah said indignantly. "You've admitted it!"

"I have. And what's more, I never did think that of him. But undeniably he was worried lest people might at least have their doubts. So, obeying a very natural impulse, he defended himself too vigorously against a charge which was never made—a fact which I'm sure he's since realised and regretted."

"That's what I mean by making mischief," Dinah said coldly.

"Do you mind explaining?" Charles requested quietly.

"Oh, what's the use?" Dinah asked impatiently. "You know perfectly well—"

"I assure you—"

"Oh, all right, then! Well, what you've just said—"

"I've just said, and not for the first time, that I don't believe Gisborne cheats," Charles said patiently. "I don't see how you can find fault with that."

"No," Dinah admitted. "But that wasn't all. You also said that he's regretted defending himself—"

"Well?"

"In other words, you're saying that he's—lacking in judgment and—and self-control. Isn't it making mischief to say that—to me, of all people?"

Charles shook his head.

"That wasn't my intention," he denied. "But even if it had been, would it have influenced you at all? You don't believe it, do you?"

"Of course I don't," Dinah insisted vehemently. "I know Nicky too well—though I suppose you don't believe that, do you? Well, all right, so we haven't known each other very long. But what of it? We *love* one another—though that's hardly likely to convince you because I shouldn't think you know very much about love, do you?"

"Very little," Charles acknowledged.

"And you think that just because we had a silly squabble then I must be talking nonsense?" she rushed on recklessly.

"I simply don't know," Charles confessed. "Since I know so little about love, how can I judge?"

"You can't—but all the same, that's just what you are doing!" Dinah declared. "So tell me, please, just what you're thinking. I want to know."

"I can't think why my opinion should interest you," Charles said rather wearily. "It's not as if you'll respect it in the least. However, if you must know, I think it doubtful if, even in a lifetime, one person ever really knows everything about another, however close the relationship may be. I think that must be so, because very few people, if any, truly know themselves."

Dinah stared at him uncertainly.

"If you mean that you don't think I—" she began, but Charles interrupted her.

"You? I wasn't thinking of you," he said harshly, and this time the weariness was unmistakable. "I was thinking about myself!"

And turning away, he went out of the room, leaving Dinah puzzled and perturbed. She was, in fact, sure of only one thing. It would be wiser not to say anything to Nicky about Charles having eavesdropped, for if she did, it could only make everything even more difficult than it already was.

At last the snow fell less heavily, though it didn't entirely stop. Charles began to feel more optimistic about getting away from Alpenglühen, though not, a telephone call to the airline offices established, of a necessity on time since there were a good many other people who had been held up ahead of him and these would naturally be given priority. However, that didn't worry Charles so long as the delay would not be too great. He had allowed himself a few days grace between arriving in London and returning to the hospital. This period could be reduced without any real inconvenience even if it was rather a nuisance.

Not such a nuisance, though, as the fact that he might have to spend an extra day or two at the hotel. The sooner he could get away, the sooner he could hope to get clear of all the complications which had so bedevilled his holiday. Consequently, when he was summoned to the telephone, his immediate reaction was one of relief, since who else than the airline was likely to be calling him?

But when he returned to the bar, it was clear from his expression that something was wrong, and Dinah felt a quick stab of apprehension as he made a beeline for the table where she and Nicky were sitting and sat down in a vacant chair.

"Hey!" Nicky protested.

"Sorry, Gisborne, but circumstances give me no choice," Charles explained crisply. "I've just had a message from the Contessa's chalet. They want me to go there at once."

"Do they, indeed?" Nicky drawled. "And just why should you imagine that we're likely to find that interesting?"

Charles ignored him and spoke directly to Dinah.

"I'm wanted because I happen to be a doctor," he went on.

The colour drained from Dinah's face and unconsciously she gripped Charles's coat sleeve.

"The Contessa—she's ill?" she whispered.

"Very ill indeed," he told her gravely. "So ill that—" And Dinah flinched because the unfinished sentence was all too significant. "She returned from Italy just before the snow began and evidently the journey was too much for her. Unfortunately her own doctor, Dr. Schwartz, is away from home, so I've been called in as the only alternative."

"So you're a doctor," Nicky shrugged indifferently. "And you've been called in to attend a titled patient. Very gratifying to you, no doubt, but as I said before, not of any interest to us!"

"Please, Nicky!" Dinah implored, and turned back to Charles.

"She wants most desperately to see you," Charles went on deliberately, but though Dinah nodded as if what he had said came as a surprise, Nicky immediately returned to the fray.

"Absolutely *not*!" he stated authoritatively. "Quite

out of the question! Do you realise that there's no hope of getting a car through the drifts? So that means a couple of miles or so on foot in appallingly difficult conditions. Why, man alive, it will take you all your time to get there, and for a girl—it's just not on. Dinah, you can't go. You must accept that."

"Apparently there's a short cut," Charles explained with what patience he could muster. "It's a pathway leading to the back of the Chalet. It's been kept reasonably clear of snow and it's unmistakably marked with tall posts and most of the way it's lit electrically. It cuts off at least a mile."

But Nicky refused to be convinced.

"Even so—" he began, and then, aggressively: "Look here, Ravenscroft, I know a damn sight more about this part of the world than you do, and I tell you, I'm not willing for Dinah to be exposed to such discomfort and, possibly, danger. And why should she be? Simply, it seems to me, to gratify the unreasonable whim of an arrogant old woman whom she hardly knows!"

Dinah didn't speak, but there was an appeal in her wide, troubled eyes which Charles knew he could not ignore.

"There is a reason—" he said slowly.

"All right, out with it, then!" Nicky challenged belligerently. "And it's got to be a good one!"

Charles hesitated momentarily. Then he took Dinah's hand firmly in his and felt her responsive grasp.

"I think you almost know without me telling you," he said gently. "The Contessa is—your mother."

In less than half an hour, they were on their way—all three of them, for though Nicky had grudgingly agreed that perhaps Dinah ought to accede to the Contessa's summons, he laid down conditions.

"I'm coming too," he announced insistently. "And what's more, until we get to the Chalet, I'm going to be the one to give the orders! I mean that, Ravenscroft, and if you want to reach your patient in anything like a reasonable length of time, you'll be wise to do as you're told."

"I agree," Charles said briefly. He would infinitely have preferred to do without Nicky's company, but he realised that not only was what he had said about understanding conditions quite true, but also that if Dinah couldn't make it, Nicky could return with her to the hotel while Charles himself continued. "I should like to start as soon as possible."

Nicky nodded and coolly took command. Charles, somewhat against his inclination, had to admit that he was the right man for the job. His orders were clear, concise and eminently practical. They covered the choice of suitable clothes and boots. He made a request for coffee in thermos flasks, biscuits and a small ruck-sack to put them into. Finally, he had a brief consultation with Emil about their route and then announced that that seemed to be the lot.

They started off under the eyes of all the intrigued visitors, to whom the unexpected excitement had made a welcome break in the monotony of the last few days, and even when the three figures were out of sight, there was still plenty to talk about—fancy Mr. Ravens-croft being a doctor! Well, of course, doctors did often keep quiet about their profession when they were on holiday, and one couldn't blame them because people *would* talk to them about their ailments—to say nothing of their operations.

But far more exciting than Charles's reticence was this extraordinary story about the Contessa being Dinah Sherwood's mother. So difficult to understand that Dinah had apparently been unaware of the fact and had to be told by Mr.—no, Dr. Ravenscroft. That was something to puzzle over—and Bébé was the one who puzzled most, though she said very little.

Dinah herself, however, had no time to think of any-thing but keeping up with the pace that Nicky was setting—they were walking in single file, Nicky leading, then Dinah herself and finally Charles. At first they were on comparatively level ground, but even so, the going was far from easy. The road leading from the hotel had been kept reasonably clear, but what was left of the snow was packed hard and was as slippery as ice. Several times Dinah's feet skidded from under her and she would have fallen but for the quick strong support which Charles gave her. But conditions underfoot were not the only difficulties with which they had to contend. The snow was only falling intermittently now, but an icy wind stung their faces and, despite the snow goggles they wore, made their eyes water.

At last they turned from the road along the pathway leading to the Chalet and their difficulties intensified. Only a narrow track had been cleared and already the wind had caused drifting which meant that several times Nicky and Charles had to get to work with the shovels they carried over their shoulders.

At these times Dinah made the most of the chance to get her breath back, but she chafed anxiously at the delay. Charles had made it very clear that no time must be wasted and her heart was full of foreboding lest they should be too late.

Strangely, she spared no thought to wonder at her own quick acceptance of Charles's revelation that the Contessa was her mother—perhaps because he had been right in saying that she had almost known without being told. But stranger still was the fact that all the bitter resentment she had felt for so long against the mother who had abandoned her with such apparent indifference had vanished as if it had never been. But about that she was only to wonder later. Her one concern now was to reach the Chalet and, despite Charles's insistence at their last halt that they should have some of the black coffee to drink, she knew that she was near the end of her endurance—and that the worst was yet to come. For now the slope of the path was steeper and they faced directly into the wind, keener now that they had left the shelter of the valley.

She was gasping with the shock of breathing the icy air and her lungs felt as if they would burst with the effort of every upward step. More than once she almost came to a halt, but each time Charles was instantly aware of her distress and his sustaining hand gripped her elbow, giving her just that extra help and encouragement that made it possible to keep going.

Then suddenly other people joined them, and supported, almost carried by two of the Chalet's outdoor staff, Dinah realised with dazed thankfulness that there was no need to struggle on any longer.

Once within the Chalet they found that everything had been thought of for their comfort. The dignified housekeeper, clucking her dismay at the sight of Dinah's condition, helped her to a bedroom where a complete change of clothes had been laid out in readiness. Dinah, quickly revived by the warmth, made a rapid change, pausing only once as, lifting one of the soft, satin garments, she was aware of the delicate perfume which emanated from it. She looked questioningly at the housekeeper, who nodded.

"Yes, they belong to the Contessa. All her clothes are so perfumed, not with scent but with sweet things from the garden. Lavender, southernwood, orris—oh, many things. Each year I gather them and fill the little bags which hang in her wardrobes and lie in her drawers. To me, it has become the essence of the dear lady herself," she concluded, tears in her eyes as she helped Dinah into the soft, quilted negligée which took the place of a dress.

Then she led Dinah to a small room where a table had been laid and where steaming bowls of soup were already in place. Nicky, but not Charles, was waiting for her. He had been provided with a somewhat miscellaneous collection of clothes which might have accounted for his evident uneasiness.

"Hallo," he greeted her gruffly. "All serene now? Then what about some grub? It smells good."

"I'd rather see the—see my mother first," Dinah told him tremulously.

"Ravenscroft's with her now," Nicky replied jerkily. "He asked me to tell you that if—it was necessary, he'd have you fetched at once, but if he didn't, he'd be glad if you'd have some food so that he didn't run the risk of having another patient on his hands. Damn cheek!" he concluded resentfully.

"No, he's quite right, Nicky," Dinah said quickly as she sat down at the table. "I must admit I don't feel like eating even though we missed lunch, but it's not my feelings that matter. There's only one thing that's of any importance just now—" and despite the aching lump in her throat, she forced herself to swallow some of the soup.

It was a silent meal, for Dinah was straining her ears to hear any sound in the quiet chalet, but apart from the maid who came in to wait on them, nothing broke the silence.

Then, suddenly, the telephone bell rang and Dinah tensed when, after a moment or so, she heard Charles speaking, though not what he actually said. Dinah waited anxiously, her eyes on the door. Surely now that Charles had been called from her mother's room he could spare just a second to let her know—

Then the door opened and Charles came in, but it was to Nicky, not Dinah, that he spoke.

"Gisborne," he began crisply, "I've just had a message from Dr. Schwartz via his surgery nurse. She can let me have a serum which both Schwartz and I feel might make all the difference. But someone will have to go and fetch it—"

Nicky jumped to his feet.

"And obviously, that someone can't be you," he interrupted coolly. "Yes, I'll go, though naturally, I can't say how long it will take me." And he glanced out of the window. The snow was falling more heavily now and the sky had darkened considerably with the heavy cloud. "Wasn't there some talk about there being lights along the path? Ask them to put them on, will you, while I change." He was halfway to the door now and in answer to a question from Charles, tossed back a reply without turning. "Oh yes, I know Schwartz's house —I've been there once or twice with minor injuries."

As soon as the door closed behind him, Dinah turned to Charles.

"Please—?" she implored anxiously.

Charles put his hands heavily on her shoulders.

"Dinah, it's no good trying to fob you off with anything but the truth," he told her grimly. "Your mother is desperately ill—and I hope to God Gisborne makes good time, because if not—" his grasp tightened. "Do you understand—and have you the courage to forget your own feelings and think only of your mother? If you can honestly tell me that you can do that, then you may come to her for you may be able to help her. But if you've any doubts, then it's better that you should keep away. Well, which is it to be? Only you can say."

Dinah, looking at the strong, stern face, saw something else that strengthened her own resolution. Here, she felt confidently, was a man who would fight his patient's battles every inch of the way. Could she do less?

"Tell me what to do," she said quietly.

"Give her hope—something to hold on to," he said vehemently. "Give her your own young strength—and the belief that life is worth living. And when you've done that, persuade her to sleep without fear. Do you understand?"

Dinah nodded silently.

"Then come," Charles said, and led the way to the Contessa's quiet room where Greta, her maid, had been left temporarily in charge. She got up when they came in and stood back for Dinah to take her place, her face blotched with weeping.

The Contessa lay propped up on pillows, frail almost to the point of transparency, so still that for a moment Dinah's own heart seemed to stop beating. Then her mother's hands moved restlessly and Dinah heard Charles say softly, "Now!" as he gave her a gentle push forward.

Dinah didn't hesitate, for there seemed to be only one thing that she could possibly do. She bent over the bed and took one of those restless hands in her own warm one and said what came instinctively to her lips.

"Mother darling!"

Instantly the Contessa's eyes opened and in them Dinah saw incredulous joy and thankfulness. She bent still lower and gently kissed the pale lips, which responded eagerly.

"I'm going to stay with you, Mother," Dinah went on steadily. "So you'll be able to rest, won't you—go to sleep if you can." She felt her mother's hand tighten very slightly on hers and knew, without being told in words, what the movement expressed. "I shall be here when you wake up. I promise you!"

The Contessa gave a little sigh of contentment, her eyelids fluttered once or twice and then closed. She seemed to relax and Dinah looked anxiously up at Charles, who was standing on the other side of the bed. He nodded reassuringly and motioned her to stay absolutely still. A few minutes later it was clear that the Contessa was sleeping peacefully and Charles came round to speak softly in Dinah's ear.

"Good girl!" he whispered. "Keep quite still for a little longer and then I'll get you a chair."

Dinah nodded silently, but she looked at Charles with a question in her eyes.

"You're giving her the best possible chance," he said softly, and just for a moment his hand rested on Dinah's shoulder in something which was almost a caress.

Time passed—just how long Dinah didn't know. Charles was as good as his word. Silently he fetched a chair and padded it with cushions so that the strain on Dinah's back and shoulders was relieved. Then he pulled up a chair for himself on the other side of the bed and neither his nor Dinah's eyes left the pale face in which, surely, there was now the faintest tinge of colour?

And still the Contessa slept, though once she stirred and her grasp on Dinah's hand tightened convulsively.

"Dinah—?" she breathed.

"I'm here, Mother," Dinah said clearly but with a tenderness that restored her mother's tranquillity. Again the Contessa slipped back into sleep and the moment slipped by.

But several times Charles glanced down at his watch and Dinah knew that he was becoming increasingly anxious for Nicky to return.

Then, at last, there was a slight stir outside the bedroom door and the unmistakable sound of Nicky's voice. Charles got up quickly and hurried over to the door. Someone must have asked a question, for Charles said grimly: "I hope so!"

Dinah's heart chilled, for she knew that could only

mean that he wasn't sure if it wasn't too late—She watched Charles anxiously as he tore open the wrappings of the little package and prepared a hypodermic syringe. Then he came over to the bedside.

"Pull up her sleeve," he ordered curtly. "Higher up— hold it like that !"

Steadily and smoothly he inserted the needle of the syringe and as steadily depressed the plunger and finally withdrew it. Then, for what seemed like an eternity, he waited, his stethoscope to the Contessa's heart.

Dinah waited in agonised silence until, at last, Charles spoke.

"A very slight response—but it's too soon yet to be sure," he warned.

Then, a little later :

"A better response. She's making a fight for it."

But it was another half hour before he gave Dinah any real assurance.

"Better than I dared hope," he told her. "Not out of danger, of course, but if she continues to improve like this, she has a good chance of turning this particular corner."

And in her relief, Dinah didn't realise the sombre significance of his concluding words. Afterwards, she understood that Charles had warned her that there were bound to be other dangerous corners for her mother and that, eventually, there would be one which she would not turn in safety.

Again there was silence. Then Charles said brusquely :

"You can get up now. Your mother will not stir for some time yet."

"I'd rather not—" Dinah began, but Charles cut ruthlessly across her protest.

"Do as you're told !" he rasped. And then, more gently : "Don't you understand, Dinah, that the next twenty-four hours are bound to be critical. Unless you're sensible, you won't be able to stand by your mother as I know you want to. So please, stand up—and hold on to the chair while you do it. You'll find you're pretty stiff if not actually cramped. That's better ! Try walking about a bit. All right? Good. And now, what about letting Gisborne know how things are? We owe him that, for he must have had a pretty rough time of it, particularly on the return journey. The snow was belting down by then and it was dark into the bargain. So what about it?"

Dinah was reluctant to go, but Charles had made his point.

"All right, I'll be sensible," she promised. "But so must you be!"

He gave her a quizzical look, but Dinah stood her ground.

"You've had no lunch," she reminded him. "And it's even more important that you should be able to keep going than that I should. If I have some food brought to you, will you promise to eat it?"

And then, for the first time in their acquaintance, Charles really smiled at her—a smile which lit up his whole face and showed a different aspect of his nature from any that she had previously known. In these last anxious hours her dislikes and doubts about him had vanished entirely, giving place to respect and trust, but now suddenly her heart warmed to him. He had become human, approachable—a really likeable man.

"Thank you, Dinah." he accepted appreciatively. "I'll be glad if you'll do that. And I promise I'll eat every scrap!"

Dinah nodded silently, looked from him to her mother's quiet face and then went in search, first of the housekeeper and then Nicky.

She found him in the room where they had lunched. He was sitting drowsing in front of the big log fire, but the slight noise of her entry roused him. For a moment he blinked owlishly at her. Then he sprang to his feet.

"Well?" he asked eagerly.

Carefully Dinah repeated what Charles had said to her. When she had finished, Nicky nodded.

"So what it comes to is that she's a little better than he'd expected her to be, but not out danger. Well, I suppose that's the best you can hope for in the meantime. A jolly good job Ravenscroft turned out to be a doctor!"

"And a good job you were here to go to Dr. Schwartz's house," Dinah said quickly. "If you hadn't been—" she shook her head significantly. "You must be absolutely exhausted!"

"Oh, hardly that!" he demurred. "A bit fagged, perhaps, but nothing that a good night's sleep won't put right."

"All the same, I'm truly grateful, Nicky," Dinah told him earnestly. "I can't tell you just how grateful."

"Oh, rot!" Nicky said awkwardly, and then, with a ruefully apologetic grin: "To tell you the truth, Dinah, if it weren't for the reason why it was necessary for me to go I'd—well, I'd have enjoyed it," he confessed. "It was a challenge, you see. And that's something that has always appealed to me, particularly when I'm playing for high stakes!"

In Dinah's present state of mind she didn't entirely take in what he had said beyond the fact that he was evidently none the worse for the effort he had made and didn't feel at all put out that Charles had made use of him as she had been half afraid might be the case.

"I'm glad," she said, smiling vaguely.

Nicky looked at her sharply, seemed on the point of saying something more and then changed his mind as a maid came in with a tea-tray which she set down on a low table near the fire.

"Oh, how nice!" Dinah said appreciatively. "Thank you—Lotta, isn't it?"

"Yes, Fräulein, I am Lotta," the girl replied with a respectful little bob. "And I am to tell you that the Herr Doktor has been fed as you wished."

"Thank you," Dinah said again, and sitting down, poured out tea for herself and Nicky. As he took his cup from her she saw that he was frowning slightly.

"What is it, Nicky?" she asked anxiously.

"I was just thinking that from the way that girl behaved it would seem that everybody here knows that you're the Contessa's daughter," he said slowly.

"I don't know—I hadn't thought about it," Dinah

134

confessed in rather a surprised way. "What makes you think they do?"

"I've told you—the respectful way the girl spoke and the little bob-curtsey she made. Don't you realise that in her eyes you're a person of considerable importance now?"

"Oh, Nicky!" Dinah protested. "I'm nothing of the sort!"

"No?" Nicky was clearly unconvinced. "But you can't deny that your mother is regarded as quite somebody, can you? So doesn't it follow—"

Dinah stood up quickly.

"Please, Nicky!" she begged, her voice shaking ominously. "Don't say things like that. They seem so unimportant when—when—" She put her fingers up to steady her quivering lips. "I must go back to her," she said hurriedly.

Nicky made no attempt to stop her, but as soon as the door closed he slumped back into his chair and stared moodily at the glowing fire.

A little later, he made a telephone call to the Hotel.

The night passed with blessed uneventfulness. Dinah, for whom a bed had been put up in the Contessa's dressing-room, woke twice and each time had crept into her mother's room to find that Charles was still on guard by the bedside. He had taken off his tie and had loosened his collar, but apart from that, had made no concessions to ease. Each time he stirred instantly as Dinah came in and had laid a finger warningly over his lips. Then, smiling, he had indicated that she should go back to bed. Dinah had gone, reassured though anxious, not so much for her mother as for Charles himself. Even in the dim light of the single shaded lamp she had seen how drawn and tired he looked and small wonder since, she was quite sure, he hadn't so much as closed his eyes during his watch. But thankful though she was for his devoted care, she knew that he could not go on indefinitely without sleep. So, gently but resolutely, she banged her head six times on the pillow and went to sleep confident that she would wake at six o'clock.

Sure enough, when next she woke, the hands of her watch told her that the childish trick had worked. She got up, washed and dressed and quietly left the dressing-room by the door which opened direct on to the landing. Her intention was to raid the kitchen for tea and perhaps something to eat for Charles and herself, but when she reached the big, pleasant room, she found that some of the staff were already on duty. She was greeted with an eager request for news of the Contessa and when she explained guardedly that Dr. Ravenscroft—how strange it seemed to call him that!—appeared to be satisfied with his patient's condition, there was a little chorus of satisfaction.

"I came down to see about making some tea for the doctor and myself," she explained a little diffidently, because the last thing she wanted to do was to appear to give orders. "And perhaps something to eat—"

Ten minutes later she returned to the dressing-room followed by a maid carrying a tray. When the girl had gone, Dinah went to her mother's room. This time, Charles's chin was sunk on to his chest and Dinah had to lay a hand on his shoulder to rouse him. Instantly he was awake and on the alert, his first reaction a searching look at the Contessa. Only when he had satisfied himself about her did he turn to Dinah. Silently she shaped the word "Tea!" with her lips and indicated the communicating door to the dressing-room with a movement of her head.

Charles got up instantly, though for a moment he stood flexing his muscles as if to make sure that he was all in one piece. Then, with a final look at the Contessa, he followed Dinah to the dressing-room, and while she poured out the tea, he stood gazing out of the window.

"No sign of it letting up yet," he remarked ruefully. "We're stuck here indefinitely, Dinah."

"Well, as far as I'm concerned, that doesn't matter," Dinah replied, handing him his cup. "I would have stayed anyhow."

"Yes," Charles said thoughtfully. "This brings a new factor into your life, doesn't it?"

She knew what he meant. How was Nicky going to react to this unexpected development and the resultant dividing of her loyalties? She had asked herself that question without finding an answer, but even so, it wasn't something she could discuss with anybody, least of all, for some reason, with Charles. That seemed to entail disloyalty to Nicky in her mind.

"Yes, it does, in a way," she admitted hurriedly. "But what I was going to say was that though being snowed up doesn't matter to me, it does to you, doesn't it?"

"Yes, I'd expected to be off tomorrow," Charles agreed. "But even if there are planes going out by then, which I rather doubt, there's quite a backlog of passengers ahead of me. I fancy I'll have to expect a delay of several days. Is there another cup in that pot?"

"Several." Dinah took his cup and refilled it. "Will it matter tremendously? If you're delayed, I mean."

"I left a few days' margin just in case," Charles told her. "I hope that'll be sufficient, but if it isn't—" he shrugged. "It's beyond my control. What I should like to happen is that Schwartz gets back before I leave so that we can discuss your mother's condition."

"Yes." Dinah braced herself. "Charles, what is going to happen?"

Charles didn't reply, but his silence answered Dinah's question. She sat very still, her hands linked loosely in her lap. For a moment Charles covered them with his hand. Then he stood up.

"And now I really must go in search of a razor," he announced, and grimaced as he rasped his fingers over his dark, rough chin. "What a scarecrow to be in a lady's boudoir! This is where Gisborne scores heavily with his beard. He'll look just as neat and trim this morning as he did yesterday, whereas I look like a tramp!"

"You look like a very tired tramp, then," Dinah told him gravely. "Charles, you've simply got to get some sleep. I'm going to make up this bed for you. Then I'll stay with Mother and call you at once if—if it's necessary."

He grinned at her quizzically, his head on one side.

"Are you by any chance bullying me?" he asked.

"I'm doing more than that," Dinah told him spiritedly. "I'm giving you an *order*—and if you've got any sense, you'll do as you're told without argument!"

"Yes, ma'am," Charles touched his forehead in a meek salute. "You're quite right, of course. It's a nuisance, but one can't go beyond a certain point without sleep. Now, I'll just have another look at your mother—"

He went into the bedroom and when he returned, he nodded reassuringly.

"She's still fast asleep and I don't think she'll stir just yet. But if she does—" He paused and laid his hands on Dinah's shoulders. "Dinah, I don't know if you realise it, but it isn't only Schwartz's drug that's helped her. It's you, my dear. You gave her happiness and peace of mind. That's why she's able to sleep so tranquilly."

"Oh, Charles, is that really true?" Dinah asked breathlessly.

"Cross my heart," he told her. "And so, when she does wake up, no matter how difficult it may be for you, I want you to do everything in your power to maintain the state of affairs."

"I promise," Dinah told him steadfastly. "You can trust me!"

"I know that!" Charles said quietly, and for a moment his hands gripped her shoulders with almost painful intensity.

Then he let her go.

"And now I really must go in search of that razor," he concluded lightly.

Dinah didn't go immediately to her mother. Charles, she knew, had wisely terminated that moment of deep emotion before it became uncontrollable, but she knew that it had left an indelible mark on her.

In some strange way she felt that Charles had transmitted some of his own unfailing strength and dependability to her and because of it, she could be sure that she would not fail her mother—or Charles.

CHAPTER EIGHT

"NO, I'm hanged if I can see why you should stay on here indefinitely," Nicky fumed. "Yes, I know the Contessa is your mother and that she's been very ill, but honestly, has she very much claim on you? She deserted you when you were a small child and she's made no effort to get in touch with you all these years. I'd have thought that you'd already done far more than she had any right to expect."

Dinah flinched at the outspoken statement. She had been obliged to explain to Nicky how it was that not until Charles had told her of the relationship had she known that the Contessa was her mother. And Nicky's reaction had been prompt and positive. He simply couldn't see her point of view in the least.

"But I've told you, it's not just because I know that my mother would like me to stay or even because I know it would be good for her if I do. I *want* to stay. Don't you understand, I felt drawn to her from the very first in a way I've never felt attracted to anyone before. It was as if we belonged—"

"That doesn't alter the fact—" Nicky began impatiently, but Dinah interrupted him.

"It *does*, Nicky. Oh, it *does*!" she insisted earnestly. "I think—I'm practically certain—that she knew who I was that day at the Schokoladhaus. I knew that in some way I mattered to her. I know it even more surely now and it makes me absolutely certain that there must, simply *must* have been a good reason why she went away and left me behind. I *know* there was!"

But Nicky was not convinced.

"It sounds a lot of nonsense to me," he told her moodily. "But have it your own way!"

They were alone together in the sitting room where Dinah, feeling more exhausted by Nicky's lack of understanding than by anything that had gone before, was sitting hunched up in front of the fire, but Nicky was wandering aimlessly about the room, pausing now and again to look without any particular interest at something which had momentarily caught his eye.

He was standing now in front of the display cabinet which housed the Contessa's treasured *bibelots*. Dinah watched as he opened the glass door and took out the little Cinderella coach. Involuntarily she stiffened. She couldn't understand why, but she felt an instinctive revulsion at seeing the dainty little piece in his strong brown hand.

"Quite a collection," he commented appraisingly. "They must be quite valuable."

"Yes, I suppose so," Dinah agreed. She got up and went over to him. "But it isn't for their intrinsic worth that Mother values them. It's because everything has a—a—"

"A sentimental value?" Nicky suggested disparagingly. "Oh, no doubt! But the fact remains, it's just one more thing, isn't it?"

"I don't understand," Dinah told him uncertainly, but driven by a compulsion she couldn't resist, she took the little coach from him and carefully replaced it. Then she shut the glass door and faced Nicky with a question in her steady eyes.

But Nicky chose to evade the issue.

"Oh, forget it!" he shrugged, and strolled over to the window to gaze out at the still whiteness. Snow was still falling with that same, unremitting persistence.

Dinah went back to her chair and waited in silence. She had said everything that there was to say without making the least impression on Nicky. He thought she was being obstinate and unreasonable, and though he had not said so in so many words, she knew that he felt her decision was a personal rebuff to him.

She could see his point of view, of course, and yet how could she leave her mother? It was true that the Contessa's condition was, as Charles had told her, very much better than he had dared to hope, but she had come slowly to realise that a real and lasting recovery was out of the question. But that was something she could not bring herself to tell Nicky. To speak of it, even to think of it, made the inevitability of the future seem nearer, more threatening. Yet ought she, in fairness, to tell Nicky?

He turned suddenly from the window.

"Dinah, I'm starting back for the hotel immediately," he announced abruptly.

"Nicky!" Dinah protested in dismay.

Nicky came and stood in front of her, his hands deep into his pockets, his head thrust aggressively forward.

"Well, why not?" he challenged. "There's no point in me staying, is there? There's nothing I can do to help."

"But for you, Mother would almost certainly be—be dead by now," Dinah reminded him unsteadily.

Nicky's shoulders shrugged dismissively.

"Oh, that! Yes, all right, I admit I came in handy then. And, to be honest, I quite enjoyed the challenge that the trip meant. But that's happened—it's in the past. There's nothing for me to do now but loaf about getting more bored and feeling more stifled with every hour that I'm here. It's not as though you spare much time to be with me, and when we are together—I don't know, Dinah, but it seems to me that you're a different girl from the one I—"

He stopped short, but Dinah knew what he had been going to say—"*A different girl from the one I fell in love with!*" And how could she deny the truth of that? So much had happened—

She swallowed convulsively.

"Nicky, are you trying to tell me that—you'd like to end our engagement?" she asked painfully.

Instantly he was all contrition, as he had been on that previous occasion when she had asked him the same question.

"Of course not!" he declared violently, and dropped on his knees beside her and put his arms round her. "I love you as much as ever—it's you that's changed. And you can't deny it, Dinah! It isn't only that you spend

141

so little time with me, I feel that you're glad of an excuse not to. Am I right?"

"No, of course you're not," Dinah denied sharply. "But—but surely you can understand—"

"Oh yes, I think I understand very well!" Nicky retorted grimly, and stood up. "My nose is out of joint, isn't it? Ravenscroft's the blue-eyed boy now, isn't he?"

"If by that you mean that I'm more grateful than I can possibly say for all that Charles has done—then yes, I am," Dinah told him steadily.

"No, I don't mean that! Oh, it may have started with gratitude, but it's developed into hero-worship—and the next stage—" his mouth twisted angrily. "Well, it's obvious, isn't it?"

"Not to me, it isn't," Dinah insisted. "And just as certainly, it isn't to Charles—"

"Oh, *him*!" Nicky dismissed Charles with utter contempt. "I don't suppose it is. He's far too much of a cold fish to feel any normal human emotions!"

Dinah didn't reply, and after a while, Nicky went on deliberately:

"Look, Dinah, we've got to face up to this. I admit that though I'll be able to make it back to the hotel, you couldn't, the way the weather is. I'll also admit, if you like, that until your mother is really better, perhaps your place is with her. But that's as far as I'll go. And that still leaves one question I'm determined to have answered. There will come a time when both the weather and your mother's health improve. I want to know what you're going to do then. Stay on here indefinitely with her—or marry me? Because, make no mistake, you can't do both! So think it over, will you, because it's up to you, you know."

And turning from her, he swung out of the room, closing the door behind him with an air of finality.

Dinah spent most of the afternoon with her mother, who was so much better that Charles had given permission for her to talk a little more than he had so far allowed.

"But mind, when I say a *little*, I mean just that!" he

warned the Contessa. "So don't forget, because if you do, I'll send that girl of yours packing!"

The Contessa's eyes twinkled as she took immediate advantage of the permission which Charles had just given.

"She wouldn't go!" she declared positively.

Charles smiled down at her.

"No, I don't think she would," he admitted. "You know—" he paused briefly, "I think you're two very fortunate people!"

"I know I am," the Contessa agreed. "In fact, I'd be perfectly happy, but for one thing—"

"My dear!" Charles said very gently.

"No, not that," the Contessa denied quickly. "That's inevitable and I've learned to accept it, as Dinah will. She will grieve, I know, but not for always. That is, if she has a full, happy life. But will she? That's what worries me, Charles. That young man—"

"Well, I suppose every mother worries when her daughter falls in love," Charles suggested matter-of-factly.

"I expect so," the Contessa agreed. "But in this case—tell me, Charles, am I wrong to feel so prejudiced?"

But Charles was not to be drawn any more than he had been on the previous occasion when she had asked him much the same question.

"That's not for me to say," he told her decisively. "And it wouldn't be of any value to you if I did, since mine is a man's point of view and so bound to differ from yours. However, it may interest you to know that Gisborne has left the chalet and has returned to the hotel."

"Yes," the Contessa said thoughtfully, "that does interest me. Do you know why he has gone?"

Charles shrugged his shoulders.

"Gisborne is essentially a man who dislikes inactivity," he remarked, still in that matter-of-fact way. "I gather that he found it irksome to be pent up here with nothing to do."

"You gathered that—from Dinah?"

"Yes."

"And did she sound unhappy about it?"

Charles considered.

"Subdued would be a better description," he said at length. "And now, Contessa, no more talking! I'll send Dinah up to you in half an hour, if you'll rest until then. But if not—" he shook his head threateningly.

"You're a bully, Charles Ravenscroft," the Contessa declared with something of Dinah's own spiritedness. "But I confess I rather like it, because you're also one of the kindest men I've ever met.

Charles gave a startled little exclamation.

"Do you know, no one's ever accused me of *that* before!"

The Contessa smiled and patted his hand affectionately.

"Perhaps you've hidden it too well—until now," she suggested, and shut her eyes with such determination that Charles knew he'd been gently but firmly dismissed, leaving the Contessa with the last word.

It would have surprised and disappointed Dinah if she had known that Charles had felt her manner to be subdued when she had told him of Nicky's departure. She had intended simply to sound matter-of-fact, and the way in which Charles had received the information had convinced her that she had succeeded.

"Sooner him than me!" he had commented feelingly, and had left it at that.

To her mother, Dinah said nothing about the matter. Had she been able to say that Nicky had phoned to say that he had reached the hotel safely, it would have been a different matter. But he hadn't and she was afraid that she might pass on her own anxiety to her mother.

For she *was* anxious. Even for a strong, experienced man like Nicky it could have been a dangerous trip and it was only natural that she should want to know that he had made it successfully. And yet she couldn't bring herself to ring up the hotel and find out. And of course

144

she knew why. It was the fact that, presuming he had got there, he hadn't bothered to ring up and tell her so.

It was confirmation, if that was needed, that a barrier had grown up between them. The barrier of sheer inability to understand each other's point of view.

Dinah tried to be honest with herself. Was she the one who was at fault? It had been so easy to fall in love and one didn't stop to ask *why*. One just revelled in happiness. But now, looking facts squarely in the face, she acknowledged that her heart's desire had been to come *first* with just one person because if that happened, then all her unhappiness of those earlier years would be wiped out. She had believed that she had come first with Nicky—and it had been wonderful—while it lasted.

She pulled herself up sharply. She wasn't being fair to Nicky. If she wanted to come first with him, wasn't it reasonable that he should have the right to expect to come first with her? And how could it seem to him that he did when she was putting her mother's needs before his?

Was love always at the mercy of conflict like this? she wondered. Could there never be compromise and if not, how did one decide who was to be the loser?

Dinah sighed. Charles, she remembered, had said that he knew very little about love. Did she know much more? There had been something else that he had said as well. That not only did he doubt whether, even in a lifetime together, two people ever got to know everything about one another, but also that his reason for saying so was that very few people ever really knew themselves. Had that been true of her, and was she only now beginning to know a little more about herself?

But whatever the answer to that might be—and she wasn't too sure that even if she knew it for certain, it would help—at least she knew one thing very certainly. If she snatched at happiness with Nicky at her mother's expense, it wouldn't be true happiness, for it would always be shadowed by self-reproach—

And now it seemed to her that she was entirely to blame for the present impasse. However much it hurt

145

to speak of it, she must explain to Nicky how tenuous
her mother's hold on life was. Then surely he'd understand—

"The weather report says that the snow will be easing
off any time now," Bébé commented idly. "That's nice,
isn't it?"

"Yes," Nicky acknowledged briefly.

He and Bébé had come into the hotel bar for a pre-
dinner drink, but Nicky wasn't enjoying his very much.
He had thought he would get rid of that feeling of
imprisonment by leaving the Chalet, but it hadn't
worked out that way. All these babbling, pleasure-
seeking folk that crowded round him gave him an even
more intense feeling of claustrophobia than the oppres-
sive luxury of the Chalet had done. There, at least,
there had been plenty of room.

"You don't sound particularly thrilled about it,"
Bébé commented. "Why not? Once the weather clears
up, all your problems will be solved!"

"Will they?" Nicky asked gloomily.

"Why, sure they will!" Bébé insisted heartily.
"You'll be able to get back to your job again, which I
imagine will be a relief to you—in fact, the season may
even be prolonged with this late fall of snow, so you'll
be at least as well off as you'd expected to be. Then—"
she went on enumerating the points on her fingers—
"you've no anxieties about a job once the season is
over, because Poppa told me this morning that he's
offered you a job."

"Yes," Nicky agreed without enthusiasm.

"You can't expect to become a colonel unless you
start as a lieutenant," Bébé told him sharply.

"No, but I'd like to feel that there's a good chance
of being a colonel before I'm too old to enjoy the
rank!" Nicky retorted, not attempting to deny Bébé's
reading of his mind.

"Oh, sure," Bébé agreed coolly. "I'm with you there!
The time to have fun is when you're young. But
look at it from Poppa's point of view. By chance he

meets a young man who's holding down a job that means he can just scrape through—"

Nicky flushed, but the description was too accurate for him to contradict it and Bébé swept on confidently.

"But he's also a young man with ambitions, and Poppa's always on the lookout for that sort. Sometimes they've got what it takes, sometimes not. Poppa feels there's only one way to find out. So he offers him a job where he can't do much harm and keeps an eye on him. Can you expect him to take a bigger risk than that?"

"I suppose not," Nicky admitted glumly. "All the same, I'm not sure he doesn't stand a chance of defeating his own ends from the very beginning!"

"Who, Poppa? How do you make that out?" Bébé asked, her eyes very wide.

"Because, though if a man settles down quite contentedly in a dogsbody job it proves that he's not fit for anything else, if he *doesn't* settle down, it isn't conclusive. It might be that he's literally good for nothing, or that, being an enterprising chap with a brain, a dull, routine job is so frustrating that he chucks it up, and goes to another firm that offers better prospects," he concluded significantly.

Bébé grinned appreciatively.

"That's very bright of you, Nicky," she conceded. "I must tell Poppa what you say. It'll interest him—though it won't make any difference. That's what he's offered and that's what he'll stick to. I know Poppa! Still, it's for you to decide. But now—" she began to count on her fingers again—"there's another thing—the most important of all, of course. Better weather and Dinah will be able to come back from the Chalet."

"If she wants to," Nicky growled.

"Oh, but surely—" Bébé began impulsively, and stopped short. "I'm sorry, Nicky. I've no right to probe into your private affairs."

"It's all right," Nicky assured her with an attempt at indifference. "It's simply that—Dinah seems to have changed—"

"Since she discovered that the Contessa is her mother," Bébé finished reflectively. "Yes, I suppose it

147

might make a difference. After all, the Contessa is quite somebody and she must be very rich—"

"That's just it!" Nicky burst out recklessly. "It was bad enough before, knowing how well off Dinah is, but now—it's stifling!"

"You don't think a wife should have much money of her own?" Bébé mused. "But is that fair on Dinah? After all, it's not her fault."

"You're very considerate of Dinah's feelings all of a sudden," Nicky said unpleasantly.

"Well, I'm in the same boat myself," Bébé explained frankly. "You see, whoever I decide to marry will do quite nicely for himself!"

"Oh, for heaven's sake!" Nicky said distastefully.

"Yes," Bébé went on dreamily as if she hadn't heard him. "You see, Poppa will be so pleased at being able to shift the responsibility for me on to someone else's shoulders that he plans to settle quite a lot of money on to my husband so that I can't boss him because I'm the one with the shekels."

"Good lord!" Nicky was amused in spite of himself. "But that's going against all the traditions about wealthy men and their prospective sons-in-law! The usual thing is for the money to be so tied up in the girl's name that her husband can't fool about with it!"

"Oh, my own money is," Bébé assured him crisply. "Make no mistake about that! And if Poppa's a bit unusual in his outlook—well, he's got his reasons. When he and Momma were married, she'd got the money and he was very small time. So that gave Momma the whip-hand—and she used it! Poppa's never said much to me about those days, but sometimes I overheard things I wasn't meant to. And one thing I remember is Poppa saying: 'Before I've finished, Paula, I'll match you dollar for dollar—and some over! Then we'll see who's boss!' Well, he did just that, and Momma had to pipe down. She didn't like it, but she knew quite well it was that or Poppa would walk out on her. Actually, he did once. She stuck it for two weeks. Then, when she realised that it was up to her whether he came back or not, she threw in the towel. There's been no real trouble since."

"Well, I can see his point of view," Nicky pondered. "And for that matter, your mother's as well. But you've got to remember one thing. Your father *earned* his money."

"Nicky Gisborne, let me tell you something!" The black eyes were both audacious and provocative. "The man who marries me will earn every penny!"

"I can well believe that!" Nicky grinned. "You'd be quite a handful! But that wasn't what I meant. Your father earned more than money. He earned your mother's respect for being able to do that. Would it be the same if you were to marry a man whose money had been a gift from your father?"

"Oh, but it wouldn't be like that," Bébé told him coolly. "There'd be strings, of course! Poppa's nobody's fool! He'd regard it as grubstaking, if you know what that means?"

"Yes, I know," Nicky acknowledged drily. "He'd expect this mythical husband of yours to put his dollars to work so that they multiplied. And if that didn't happen—"

"He'd be out!" Bébé declared emphatically. "He'd never touch so much as another cent of Poppa's money. Or of mine," she added softly.

Nicky didn't answer. He was, in fact, beyond speech, for he felt as if all the breath had been knocked out of him.

He knew perfectly well what Bébé was driving at. She meant to make it quite clear that he had only to ask her to marry him for her to fall into his arms—but it would be on her terms.

For a moment he was furiously angry. So she thought he'd got his price, did she? Well, he'd soon show her—

Then, abruptly, his mood changed as he realised that here at last was an opportunity such as he had never thought would come his way. It was a challenge, too, a challenge that would make tremendous demands on every ounce of ability he'd got. Every fibre of his being

149

stirred with a sense of exhilaration. This was what he'd been on the lookout for all his mature life—and this confounded girl knew it.

"You little devil!" he said very softly.

Triumph flashed in Bébé's eyes, but it passed so quickly that Nicky was not even sure he had seen aright, for those same eyes became limpid and guileless.

"Not really," she denied with a hint of wistfulness. "Just—I think it's a good idea to find out what you really want—and then go bald-headed for it. Don't you?"

Well, did he, or didn't he? Nicky hesitated. Then, abruptly, he got up and strode out of the bar.

A good many things happened in the next few days. The airport became usable again and Dr. Schwartz was able to return to Alpenglühen. He and Charles had a consultation about the Contessa, the outcome of which was that Dr. Schwartz approved everything that Charles had done and made this quite clear to Dinah.

"We have been very fortunate in having the services of a man with Dr. Ravenscroft's outstanding qualifications available," he told her. "But for him—" he shook his head significantly.

"He's been wonderful," Dinah replied warmly. "So kind and understanding and—and strong."

The look which Dr. Schwartz gave her held both curiosity and interest.

"I am very glad to hear you say that," he said with an emphasis which passed over Dinah's head. "He also speaks very highly of the part which you have played."

"I've truly tried to do my best," Dinah said earnestly. "But I couldn't have done it without Dr. Ravenscroft's backing."

Dr. Schwartz nodded understandingly.

"But now, very soon, Dr. Ravenscroft must leave," he reminded her. "And I, though I will of course do everything in my power to care for the Contessa, will not always be at hand."

Dinah's heart sank. Of course she had known that Charles would be going, but only now had she realised what that meant. Dr. Schwartz was a kindly man and she had taken a liking for him, but he wasn't Charles, with whom she had battled for her mother's life. How could she get on without his comforting presence? But of course, she'd got to—

"I could, if you would provide a nurse or nurses," Dr. Schwartz suggested, noting her hesitation.

"Only if you think that's really necessary," Dinah said earnestly. "If you don't, and you think that with Greta's help I can manage, then I think Mother would be happier without—without—"

"Without too much emphasis being laid on her invalidism." Dr. Shwartz nodded his agreement. "Yes, I think you are right, Miss Sherwood." Again he looked at her with that deep interest. "How long do you intend to stay with the Contessa?"

"As long as she needs me," Dinah said steadily.

For she had made up her mind about that now. As soon as it had been possible, she had had a letter taken down to Nicky. It wasn't very long. Simply she told him how serious her mother's condition was and that she was sure that, knowing that, he would understand that she must stay on.

As it happened, her letter crossed one from Nicky in which he told her of Mr. Vallaise's offer and his own acceptance of it.

"This is a chance I'm unlikely ever to have again," he wrote. "It could lead to almost anything. And that means that I can't afford to turn it down. Don't you see, Dinah, it makes our happiness possible *now,* so is it any wonder that I don't want there to be thousands of miles separating us?"

That letter she hadn't answered, for she was quite sure that when Nicky had read hers, he would write again—as he did. But what he wrote was not what she thought it would be.

"I'm sorry about your mother, but are you sure it's true? I mean, doctors can make mistakes, and these days, with all the new drugs, surely something can be done for her. In any case, even if it's true, don't you see what an impossible situation it is? It *may* only be a question of a few months, but that isn't certain, is it? It may go on for years—one does hear of such cases.

"Quite honestly, Dinah, I'm forced to the conclusion that you're using this as an excuse. To me it's evident that I'm no longer of any importance to you—sometimes I wonder if I ever really was. So for heaven's sake be honest with me. Either marry me now—or admit that you've changed and want your freedom, which, of course, you can have. I'm not the sort of chap to keep a girl tied against her will."

Dinah's hands were shaking as she put the letter down. So that was the real Nicky! Callous, self-centred and utterly determined not to let anything or anybody even temporarily stand between him and what he wanted.

But even that was not all. Reading between the lines, it was quite clear that it was Nicky who wanted his freedom, but he wouldn't admit it, even to himself. Why else, despite that last appeal of hers, had he remained so obstinately unconvinced of the truth? Because he didn't want to be convinced. Could that mean anything else than that, much as he wanted his freedom, he didn't want to accept the responsibility of making the break because to do so would damage his self-esteem? So, instead, he accused her of being the one who had changed.

And this was the man she had believed she loved! She shivered violently as something which had been very lovely shrivelled and died in her. Something which could never be recreated—first, enchanted love.

With a sudden revulsion of feeling, she scrumpled the hateful letter and flung it into the fire. Then, slowly but deliberately, she drew Nicky's ring from her finger.

"You know," Charles said with a sigh of sheer repletion, "I think the staff must be thoroughly glad to be getting rid of me tomorrow!"

"I'm sure they're not," Dinah declared. "Whatever makes you think that?"

For the last few evenings they had dined together

and now, with the meal finished, were enjoying their coffee in the sitting room.

"Well, the meal they put on tonight," Charles explained. "Admittedly, Cook's standard is always high, but tonight it's really been out of this world! As if the staff feel that they've had something to celebrate—me going, in fact!"

Dinah smiled. She realised that Charles must at least suspect that her engagement to Nicky had ended. Her ringless finger made that clear, and though she had, she hoped, shown no sign of distress when she was with her mother, it hadn't been easy to keep up appearances all the time. In fact, if it hadn't been for Charles she wouldn't have succeeded as well as she had. He had asked no questions, offered no sympathy. Simply, he had behaved as if nothing out of the way had happened and so, she had not had to be on the defensive. Nothing could have been more helpful and she had done her best to respond to his tactfulness.

"I'm sure that wasn't the reason," she told him positively. "I think it was by way of being a special 'thank you' for all that you've done for Mother. They're all very fond of her, you know."

"I know they are—and small wonder. The Contessa is a very easy person to become fond of—and to trust," he added thoughtfully.

Dinah looked at him intently, alert to his sudden gravity.

"You said that for some special reason, didn't you?" she asked.

"Yes, I did," he acknowledged. "Dinah, do you know how much happiness it has given your mother that you've, so to speak, taken her on trust without asking questions about her past—and yours?"

"Has it? I'm glad," Dinah said simply. "Very, very glad. But it's really her doing, you know. Because now that I've found her, I know that she wasn't to blame. She couldn't have been!"

And Charles didn't argue about that as Nicky had done.

"I quite agree with you," he declared emphatically. "And I'm speaking with the knowledge of what actually happened."

"You are?" Dinah exclaimed, startled. "But how? Did Mother tell you?"

"Yes. Some time ago," he admitted, and without pausing to give her any chance of asking any more questions, he went on: "Which is perhaps just as well because she wants you to know and since it is a fairly long story, it would take rather an effort for her to tell you herself. So—?" he looked enquiringly at Dinah.

"If Mother wants me to know," Dinah agreed. "But I'm quite content to leave things as they are if she'd rather."

"But she really wants you to know," Charles repeated. "You see, she still blames herself, and I think that if, knowing, you can forgive her—or feel that there's nothing to forgive, it will ease her mind."

"In that case—" Dinah murmured, unconsciously tensing herself for what was coming.

Very simply, using, so far as he could remember them, the Contessa's own words, Charles recounted the old, unhappy story and Dinah listened in silence, very still, never taking her eyes off his face. Once or twice, tears gathered and slid unchecked down her cheeks, and when he had finished, she sighed deeply.

"Yes, I've thought—lately—that it must have been something like that," she said in a low voice. "Poor darling, how desperately unhappy she must have been. She's such a warm, outgoing sort of person. He—my father—must have frozen her just as he did me. He just didn't care about other people's feelings, you know. I don't think it ever occurred to him that they might have any because he hadn't himself. Do you think there are many men who are like that? Who put things like ambition and success before people?"

"Some," Charles said briefly, his hand before his eyes as if to shield them from the fire.

"Then I'm sorry for them," Dinah said emphatically. "They miss so much! Oh, I know, being warmhearted made Mother vulnerable." As it did me, she might have

154

added. "But to be so hard and unfeeling that you're locked away from the rest of the world—that's terrible. It means that you're less than a whole person—less than real."

Charles was startled. At the Contessa's request, he had not repeated what she had said about Esmond Sherwood's lack of humanity and humility, but here was Dinah saying much the same thing though in different words.

"I think you're right," he agreed. "But, rather oddly, that isn't quite the end of the story. Your father's fault wasn't ambition in the worldly sense. It was his work and his total absorption in it that made him what it was. As I've told you, your mother said that he was the sort of man who should never have married, and I think she was right. None the less, but for that utter devotion to his work—" he leaned forward as if to lay emphasis on what he was about to say. "Dinah, the drug that has pulled your mother through is one which your father's research made possible. But for his work—"

Dinah drew a deep breath.

"I'm glad of that," she said slowly. "I don't know why, because really it doesn't make any difference—and yet it does."

"That's why I told you—and by the way, I'm leaving you to tell your mother when you see fit. And now—" he stood up, "I'm going to have a little chat with her in case she's sleeping when I have to leave tomorrow."

But on the point of leaving the room, he suddenly turned.

"Dinah, I wish I didn't have to go," he said impulsively.

"I wish you didn't, too," Dinah confessed, her lips quivering.

Just for a moment their eyes met and held. Then, without speaking again, Charles went out of the room.

Early the next morning, he left.

CHAPTER NINE

LIFE at the Chalet became a tranquil routine which nothing was allowed to disturb. If there were any problems, either the staff dealt with them or Dinah was consulted. At first she had been loath to give orders, but it soon became evident that it was not only expected of her, but that no one resented her assuming authority, with the possible exception of Greta. She did, perhaps, resent the fact that she was no longer solely responsible for the Contessa's personal comfort, but having come to the conclusion that Dinah's presence was preferable, from her point of view, to that of professional nurses, she co-operated willingly enough so that the peaceful happiness which surrounded the Contessa was not broken.

Gradually, the snows receded until only the peaks of the mountains retained their white caps.

Spring had come and Dinah, sharing it with her mother felt that she had never seen anything so beautiful in her life before. The grass was so green, the flowers so gay and the many little streams, the product of the melting snow, seemed to chuckle with delight as if they were enjoying their new-found freedom.

And Dinah herself was happy, not only because of the beauty which surrounded her but because her mother was able now to be up for part of the day, and though she tired very quickly, there was no doubt about it, she had made an amazing recovery. And that, Dinah knew, was because she was happy. That terrible burden of guilt had been lifted from her now that Dinah knew the whole story and had convinced her that her own hurt had faded into the past.

Of Esmond Sherwood they spoke little—the Contessa because, no matter what she had suffered through his cold, unsympathetic nature, she was determined not to add to Dinah's own unhappy memories of her father or to seek to excuse her own actions by blaming him.

This last was perhaps due to the fact that Dinah had told her of the coincidence of his connection with the drug which had proved so efficacious for the Contessa's response had been almost exactly the same as Dinah's own. Logically, the fact really made no difference to what had happened in the past, and yet it brought a certain satisfaction and forgiveness.

"I don't know if it's because it's made me feel that his devotion to his work was justifiable or whether it's just that there are some things—perhaps the most important things—which are beyond logic or reason," she confessed. "But whichever it is, I'm glad about it."

And there they were content to leave it. Nor did the Contessa speak very much about her second husband, though the little that she did say made it very clear how deep their love for one another had been—and what a very different man he had been from Esmond Sherwood.

"I wish I'd known him," Dinah said impulsively once. "He sounds as if he was a dear!"

"He was," the Contessa said briefly, but with a warmth which spoke for itself. "And I wish you could have met. But though that's impossible, you will soon be meeting someone who is very, very much like him—his son by his first marriage—another Guido."

And so, for the first time, Dinah learned that she had a stepbrother who was happily married and who had two delightful children. What was more, he had written to the Contessa to say that, if she felt up to it, he would come to see her the following week.

"Literally, I'm afraid, a flying visit," he wrote. "Since, as you know, I'm a busy man. But I want not only to satisfy myself that all is well with you, but also to meet my little sister at long last. Lucia and the children insist that I must bring my camera so that I am able to bring back pictures of her—"

"They sound kind—and family-ish," Dinah commented as the Contessa folded the letter up.

"They are just that," the Contessa nodded. "A warmhearted little family circle which will gladly open to include you. You've got a family now, darling!"

As for Nicky, they didn't speak of him at all, once Dinah had told her mother that she had broken off the engagement and that she would rather not talk about it. She had heard nothing more from him—indeed, she had neither expected nor wanted to. Nothing, she knew, could bring them together again, and if she couldn't forget, at least she could do her best not to dwell on the memory of the happiness which had proved to be so transient. In fact, it turned out to be less difficult than she had anticipated, for so completely absorbed did she become in her present circumstances that it became increasingly difficult to credit that she had been that other girl. It seemed more as if her romance was something which had happened to someone else, or that she had read about in a book, so completely unreal had it become. She didn't try to analyse how this had come about, but there was no doubt about it, Nicky's image was steadily fading. And if, at times, she looked thoughtfully at the finger which had worn his ring, it was in wonder that it had ever been there rather than regret that it no longer was.

None the less, it was a relief when Frau Emil, who came to see the Contessa whenever she could spare time, remarked casually that all the winter visitors had now left and that they would shortly be welcoming the summer ones. That meant that Dinah could now go down to Alpenglühen without the possibility of meeting either Nicky or any of the other visitors who knew what had happened. Charles, in fact, was the only link left with that past existence. Before leaving the Chalet he had asked Dinah if she would write to him with news of her mother, and Dinah had promised to. Her first letter had been brief and Charles's reply had not been very much longer, but gradually, over the weeks, they had found more to say to one another. Charles would sometimes tell her about a patient—it might be an amusing incident or, in a more serious vein, his satisfaction when a patient about whom he had almost given up hope had responded to a new treatment. In reply, Dinah would tell him about Alpen-glühen—its new beauty now that spring had come. To that Charles's reply had been nostalgic :

"I wish I could see it all as you describe it. One day, I promise myself that I will. But in the meantime, your description has been almost as refreshing and invigorating as if I were standing beside you sharing it all. Almost—but not quite."

That letter, for some reason, Dinah read several times over.

By the same post she had another letter from London, this time from Ellen Joliffe. Her wedding had been put forward a month because her fiancé, Euan Forbes, who worked for a big chemical firm, had been un-expectedly posted overseas.

"He'll be in Canada for six months and then go on to Japan for another three," Ellen wrote. "And since I can go with him, it seems stupid to postpone our wedding. Oh, Di, it's all frightfully exciting ! We're living in an absolute *whirl* of activity with only Mother keeping her head ! Even so, Father is talking about emigrating until it's all over, or at least going fishing in Norway. And I think he might have done that, only Euan, bless him, has tactfully whisked him off to Scotland to stay with an uncle who has a wonder-ful stretch of river simply chock full of salmon. After landing two good sized ones, Father wrote quite amiably to Mother and enclosed a nice fat cheque for my trous-seau which has sort of overflowed what Mother had told him it would be.

"And now, Di, about you being my chief bridesmaid. Mother warns me that you may not want to leave the Contessa and, darling, I do understand, honestly I do. But I *do* want you, if it's in any way possible.

"Actually, you wouldn't need to be away so very long. The wedding is on June 4th. If you were to catch an evening flight on the 3rd and return on a morning flight of the 5th, you'd be away for less than forty-eight hours.

"And then, about your dress—we're so much of the

same size that if it fits me, it'll be all right for you, so there's no bother there.

"So what about it, Di?"

But before she had half finished the letter, Dinah had made up her mind. She had looked forward to Ellen's wedding and she was truly sorry to disappoint her old friend, but no, she didn't want to leave her mother for even that comparatively short time. But though she was quite definite about that, the letter refusing was never written, for the Contessa had also heard about the change of plans—from Mrs. Joliffe. And she took it for granted that, naturally, Dinah must go.

"It will be great fun for you," she insisted. "And you needn't worry about me, because I shan't be alone. Guido has written to me again saying that if he postpones his visit for a week or two, he can stay longer. I was going to agree to that anyhow, but since it partly coincides with the time you'll be away, it fits in perfectly. You and he will have a few days getting to know one another and he'll still be here when you return. So write to Ellen and tell her you're coming—and make your plane reservations. Yes, really, darling. I mean it!"

Even so Dinah would have felt that she must refuse until it occurred to her that perhaps, really, her mother would prefer it this way. It would give her an opportunity for having her stepson to herself without the presence of someone about whom they were quite sure to want to talk.

The intervening days passed with incredible speed until, at the end of May, Guido Farini arrived. Dinah liked him at sight. Always afterwards, she thought of him as a big brown man with his sunburnt face and dark hair; her second impression was of the innate kindliness which found expression in his sensitive mouth and smiling eyes.

"If his father was like him, then I don't wonder—" she thought as he took her two hands in his and smiled down at her.

"So this is my little sister," he said warmly. "I can't tell you how glad I am to meet you at last! And even more that you and your mother have found one another.

160

You have given her greater happiness than anyone else in this world could have done! And you? You are happy, Dinah?"

"Yes, I am," she told him unhesitatingly. "Or—or I would be if it weren't—" and her eyes filled with tears.

"Ah yes." Guido Farini put his arm comfortingly round her shoulders. "But that we will not think of now, will we? We will all be happy together for the sake of our beautiful little mother."

"You're very fond of her, aren't you?" Dinah said unsteadily.

"Very fond indeed," Guido confirmed simply. "Both for what she herself is and for the happiness she gave my father—a greater happiness than he had ever known in his life before. And that is why, for their sakes as well as for your own, little sister, I want you to know that, come what may, you need never again feel that you are alone in the world. Remember that!" And momentarily his arm tightened round her. "And now," he went on cheerfully, "may I see the little mother? But first, I must unpack the gifts that my wife, Lucia, and the children have sent."

And so, when he went to the sitting room, his arms were piled high with odd shaped parcels and packages. The Contessa laughed softly as she greeted him.

"You look like Father Christmas, Guido dear," she told him.

"And you, *cara mia*, look like the fairy on the top of the Christmas tree!" he retorted as he set down his burdens and bent to kiss her.

Dinah slipped quietly away leaving them together, and for the first time since she had agreed to go to England for the wedding, her conscience was at ease. Her mother would be both safe and happy with Guido there.

None the less, when the day came for her to leave, she was the prey of last-minute doubts and fears. She turned to her stepbrother, who was seeing her off at the airport, and caught hold of his sleeve.

"Guido, if—if anything should happen, you will let me know *at once*, won't you?" she begged.

"Yes, I will," he promised unhesitatingly. "And in any case, I will ring you up tonight, tomorrow morning and evening and again before you return the following morning. That is a promise! What is more, I believe I shall have good news for you each time. So enjoy yourself with your friends, Dinah, so that you may have many happy things to tell the little mother when you return!"

And once she was with the Joliffes it really was impossible not to enter into the excitement and the atmosphere of festivity that prevailed. Mrs. Joliffe greeted her affectionately and asked after her mother.

"We'll have a long talk tomorrow," she promised. "But now, you really must let Ellen show you her dress and yours, because I think she'll probably explode if she doesn't. And you'd better try yours on, dear, just to make quite sure."

It turned out to be just as well that she had said that, for the dress didn't fit quite as well as Ellen had so confidently anticipated.

"Either I've got fatter or you've got thinner," she pronounced cheerfully. "Oh well, there's plenty of time to take in a few reefs!"

But afterwards, to her mother, she confided that actually Dinah was the one who had altered.

"She's terribly thin, Mother," she said anxiously. "It was all I could do not to let her see how upset I was."

"It's hardly to be wondered at," Mrs. Joliffe pointed out. "Poor child, she's been under great emotional stress, you know. And not only on account of her mother, I fancy. Didn't you tell me that she'd met a young man in whom she seemed very much interested?"

"Yes, I did," Ellen replied. "In fact, she was so full of him that I thought from the way she wrote they were actually engaged, though she didn't say so in so many words. But she isn't wearing a ring, and what's more, she hasn't said a word about him to me."

Mrs. Joliffe laughed.

"Darling, have you given her much chance to talk about anything except your wedding?" she teased.

"No, perhaps I haven't," Ellen agreed with a grin. "It *is* rather filling my mind just now! Still, I've got time to wish that Di was as happy as I am—not that anyone could be, quite—and she's not. I mean, if there was a nice young man in the background, I don't think even her distress about her mother would make her so— so—withdrawn. Because that's what she is. Oh, not on the surface. She's careful to seem just as she always was. But that's just it. She's on her guard all the time. And that's what I don't like."

Nor did Mrs. Joliffe, for Ellen had confirmed her own first impressions. Still, there was nothing that could be done about it for the moment, she thought, as she went off to deal with just one more problem that must be settled if everything was to go smoothly the next day. But she made up her mind that no matter how tired she might be when it was all over, she must see to it that she had a talk with Dinah. She wouldn't ask any awkward questions, of course, but she would give her every chance to unburden herself if that was what she needed.

Ellen's day dawned bright and fair, and when, very early, she came bursting into Dinah's room, there was a radiance about Ellen herself which even an ancient dressing gown and lack of make-up couldn't dim.

"Darling, you look absolutely wonderful!" Dinah exclaimed, hugging her friend.

"What, in this rig?" Ellen laughed. "More like something left over at a jumble sale! Mother says practically everything I've been wearing for the last month is going straight into the rag bag! Oh, Di, isn't it a lovely day!"

"Well, of course it is," Dinah sounded as if she was surprised that there should be any question about that. "Your mother made all the arrangements, didn't she? So naturally she wouldn't forget to order a specially good day!"

Ellen giggled appreciatively and the two girls settled down to the serious business of the day. Then Guido rang up and his report was so reassuring, as his overnight one had been, that Dinah was able to relegate her own concerns to the background and identify herself with Ellen's.

She made a lovely bride, partly, of course, because the traditional bridal white can make the best of even a plain girl—and Ellen was far from that. But that radiant look which Dinah had seen in her friend's face early that morning now had a raptness added to it which was utterly enchanting. There was no doubt about it, Ellen was following her heart. And Euan, too, when they reached the church, had the quiet confidence of a man who had no doubts about the future.

They were so sure of each other, Dinah thought with a little pang as she remembered how sure she had been about Nicky and herself. And yet she had been wrong. They certainly had not been made for one another. How could one make mistakes like that? But this wasn't the time to think about that. Perhaps one should never dwell on past mistakes—and yet, having once been so blind, how could she ever trust herself to know for sure that if—and what a big "if" it was!—another man came into her life it was the real thing!

The reception was fun. A big marquee had been put up in the garden, but because it was such a splendid day, the walls of it had been rolled up so that only the roof of it was left to give shade and guests could wander out into the garden at their will.

Dinah found herself always forming part of a gay little group of the younger guests who had, although she didn't know it, been delegated by Ellen to see that she never felt out of it since she didn't know many people. But that had really hardly been necessary. Dinah's own charm was sufficient to attract attention—and hold it—particularly where the male sex was concerned. True, the best man, traditionally her partner for the occasion, happened to be engaged and hadn't much time to spare for anyone but his fiancée, but his younger brother more than made up for his defection.

He was a cheerful, lighthearted young man who, in the space of a few minutes, skilfully cut her out from the rest of the crowd and installed her in a cool, secluded corner of the garden. He also proved to be an adept at securing a tray full of food and drink and while they dealt with it, set himself to amusing her. Dinah found herself laughing at his nonsense as she hadn't laughed for a long time, and encouraged by this, he was quick to take her into his confidence and pour out his troubles to her.

"You're so sympathetic," he told her with such gravity that she wasn't too sure if he was serious or not, but she listened intently just in case he was.

It soon appeared that his troubles weren't very serious ones, simply, she quickly realised, he was the sort of happy-go-lucky soul who would be in and out of mischief all his life. His name, he told her, was Bobby Wilson and he was a second year medical student. This was said so mournfully that Dinah asked him why.

"Do you wish you'd chosen something else?"

"No, not really," he said. "At least, I can't think of anything else I'd rather do. Only it's so *slow*. Getting on and doing anything really interesting. One just gets all the dogsbody jobs when what I'd really like—"

"I know," Dinah interrupted, her eyes alight with amusement. "You would like for there to be an emergency and only you available to save the life of a beautiful girl who turned out to be the daughter of a millionaire, who, naturally would be grateful."

Bobby stared at her open-mouthed.

"How did you know?"

"Oh, I was young myself once!" Dinah told him lightly.

"You still are," Bobby said enthusiastically. "And awfully pretty. Do you mind me telling you so?"

"Not in the least," Dinah said cheerfully. "But do you think, instead of paying me compliments, you could get some more food? I'm absolutely starving—we had a very early breakfast, you see."

"No soul," Bobby grumbled. "Just like all the rest of them—and I thought you were different. Oh well, I must say I'm a bit peckish still myself!"

He came back a little later with a laden tray, but he

looked so downcast that, anxiously, Dinah asked if there was anything wrong.

"I'll say," he told her gloomily. "One of our big white chiefs is here. He's tied up talking to the Joliffes at present, but sooner or later he's bound to circulate, and I'm scared!"

"Oh?" Dinah helped herself to a tempting cake. "Why?"

"Because though naturally one expects to have to toe the line where the pundits are concerned, the Raven's a holy terror! Bite your head off as soon as look at you!"

"The Raven?" Dinah repeated sharply. "Do you happen to mean Charles Ravenscroft?"

Bobby's jaw dropped.

"Oh, my lord, do you know him?" he asked dismally. "Trust me to put my foot in it!"

"Don't be silly," Dinah advised him severely. "And stop looking so scared. There can't be any question of him snubbing you on a social occasion like this. You're both guests—absolute equals."

"Oh yes?" Bobby retorted sceptically. "Well, I don't feel like it. More like a kid caught scrumping apples by a policeman!"

"Oh, rubbish!" Dinah said impatiently. "Of course I know what you mean. At the hospital, he's important and you're not. But this isn't the hospital, and Charles would never embarrass his host and hostess by snubbing another guest!"

"Well, you may be right at that," Bobby agreed, although without much conviction. "Though you wouldn't have been, not so very long ago. Talk about being upstage and standoffish! Why, he hadn't got a single pal in the hospital even among his colleagues, and as for us embryo medicos, we were just the lowest form of life—far too low for him even to be aware of his existence!"

"Be quiet!" Dinah stormed in a fierce undertone. "I won't listen! It's horrible to talk like that behind someone's back and I don't blame Charles for ignoring you. You're not worth noticing!"

166

"Here, I say!" Bobby protested in an injured voice. "I only told you because, well—he does seem to have changed quite a bit lately. Since he came back from a holiday in Switzerland, in fact." He looked at Dinah in sudden speculation, but her face was hidden by the big-brimmed hat she was wearing. "He's more approachable. More human, if you know what I mean."

He was rewarded by a flashing smile to which he instantly responded. Then his face dropped.

"He's making a beeline for us," he said apprehensively under his breath. "I think, if you don't mind, I'll push off—"

But he was too late. Charles had already joined them. He smiled at Dinah and gave Bobby a friendly nod.

"Having a good time, Wilson?" he asked pleasantly.

"Yes, thank you, sir. Splendid," Bobby assured him rapidly. And then, to Dinah: "If you'll excuse me—"

"Of course," Dinah said matter-of-factly, and Bobby scuttled off. But he couldn't resist the temptation to turn and they saw that his expression was a mixture of relief and amazement.

"Now what's the matter with him?" Charles wanted to know. "He looked as if he'd seen a ghost!"

"He thought you'd be sure to bite him—and he was almost more put out that you didn't than if you had," Dinah explained gravely.

Charles sat down beside her, but he didn't make any reply. And Dinah felt suddenly shy and tongue-tied. Perhaps it was because, listening to Bobby she had, really for the first time, realised that Charles was an important person in his own world. Or it might have been that Charles, in formal garb, seemed a very different person from the man she had known in Alpenglühen. More imposing and—aloof? Or was he, in these different circumstances, feeling that she was something of a stranger?

"I didn't know you knew the Joliffe's," she said at length, desperately anxious to break the silence.

"I didn't, until now," he explained carefully. "I was invited on Euan's account. We're vaguely related—two or three times removed cousins is the nearest we've

167

ever been able to work it out. But we've always been good friends. In fact, I would have been his best man only I'm such an unreliable cove that we decided it wasn't on. Just as well, because I couldn't get away in time to be at the church."

"Oh, I see," Dinah murmured. "Ellen and I were at school together. Did you know?"

"Only very recently," Charles replied, still in that rather oddly precise way. "Quite a coincidence, isn't it?" But then, without waiting for her reply, he changed the subject. "How is your mother? Reasonably well, I imagine, since otherwise you would hardly have left her."

"I wouldn't have done anyhow if Guido weren't staying at the Chalet," Dinah said defensively, feeling that his choice of words suggested that he might be reproaching her for leaving her mother.

"Guido?" Charles said sharply.

"Mother's stepson," Dinah explained. "My stepbrother. They're very fond of one another—and I think, perhaps, that Mother will enjoy having him to herself for a day or two. It will make it easier for them to talk about things—including me."

"Quite," Charles agreed absently. "Your stepbrother —is he married?"

"Oh yes. Very happily, I think. They have two children—a boy and a girl." She paused momentarily and then, because Charles still seemed to be waiting for more information, she went on: "Guido has been very kind and—and brotherly to me. He and his wife, Lucia, want me to go and stay with them—some time."

She didn't have to explain what that meant, but Charles answered as if she had.

"Schwartz has very decently written to me several times," he told her. "He's delighted with the improvement in your mother's condition, as I expect he's told you."

"Yes, he has," Dinah agreed. "But all the same—" she broke off, her face turned from him.

Charles laid his hand over hers and for a moment neither of them spoke. Then Charles broke the silence.

"Dinah, I want you to promise me something," he told her with an impulsiveness which she found strange in him.

"Yes?" she said wonderingly.

"I want you to promise me that if ever you need me, if ever I can be of use to you, you'll let me know."

"And you'd come, Charles?" she asked. "Even if, like today, your work had prior claim?"

He didn't hesitate.

"Unless a life depended on me being here, yes, I'd come."

"Thank you, Charles," Dinah said softly.

They didn't have any further opportunity of talking together. First they had to join the other guests in the marquee for the speeches, then more photographs were taken, and finally Dinah had to help Ellen change into her going-away clothes.

"What a perfect day!" Ellen breathed blissfully, standing in front of her mirror for a last glimpse of herself in her wedding finery.

Without comment, Dinah, standing behind her, smiled into her friend's reflected eyes. Ellen turned quickly.

"Di, you have enjoyed yourself, haven't you?" she asked anxiously.

"Yes, I have," Dinah said unhesitatingly. "To be quite honest, Ellen, far more than I'd thought it would be possible for me to."

"I'm glad," Ellen said simply, giving her friend a warm hug. "That makes me feel not such a beast for twisting your arm a bit, about coming."

"Oh, but you didn't do that," Dinah protested, laughing.

"Well, I don't know so much. Actually, I got Mother to write to your mother about you being my bridesmaid because I was afraid that you'd simply say 'no' without telling her anything about it."

"That's what I'd intended to do," Dinah admitted slowly. She wished that Ellen hadn't told her this, for it made her feel that her mother—and she herself, for that matter—had been subjected to undue pressure.

169

And then another, even less pleasing idea occurred to her. "Did Charles know that your mother was writing?"

"Charles?" repeated Ellen vaguely, her voice muffled because she was pulling her going-away dress over her head. "Charles—who?"

"Ravenscroft," Dinah explained, regretting that she had asked the question.

"What's he got to do with it?" Ellen wanted to know as she emerged from her dress.

"He was staying at the Tannenhof while I was there," Dinah explained, wishing more than ever that she had held her tongue since Ellen's round-eyed surprise made it clear that this was news to her. "He was the doctor who looked after Mother because her own doctor was away."

"Did he, though!" Ellen exclaimed with considerable interest. "I didn't know that. What an extraordinary coincidence!"

"You didn't know?"

"Not until this minute. And I shouldn't think Mother did either. I mean, doctors just don't discuss their patients with other people, do they? And I should think Charles is even more of a stickler over that sort of thing than most of them would be. Oh, my hair! I have messed it up!"

Giving all her attention to restoring her hair to order, Ellen lost all interest in the subject, much to Dinah's relief. After all, quite apart from the fact that it was probably true that Charles had rigid ideas about professional conduct, he had categorically said not only that until today, he hadn't known the Joliffes, but also that it was only very recently that he had known of the friendship between Ellen and herself. So it must be simply a matter of coincidence. Such things did happen—

In the excitement and bustle of Ellen's and Euan's departure, Dinah forgot everything else, particularly as, when at the very last moment, Ellen tossed her bridal bouquet out of the car window, it was she who caught it. As a result, blushing furiously, she became the centre of a good-natured, laughing crowd of guests who assured her that she would be the next to get married.

Then, though everyone else went back to the marquee, Dinah stood where she was, silently regarding the lovely flowers she held. Herself the next bride! She could hardly think of anything less likely!

"That's rather a charming superstition, isn't it?" Charles's voice said behind her. She wheeled sharply.

"Yes, isn't it?" she agreed equably, and then found herself adding, almost against her will: "Though not always likely to be fulfilled!"

"No?" He took her bare left hand in his and regarded it thoughtfully. Then, quite deliberately, he looked at her with an unmistakable question in his dark eyes.

"That is over," she said steadily. "Quite over and done with!"

"I see," he said briefly, and let go of her hand. When he spoke again, it was to tell her that he was leaving at once.

"Oh, I'm sorry, Charles," Dinah said disappointedly. "I'd hoped that we could have had a longer talk together."

"I'd have liked that," Charles admitted. "But—" he shrugged his shoulders. "That's how it is with my job. It frequently has to take precedence over one's personal wishes."

"Yes, of course," Dinah murmured, remembering that this wasn't the first time he'd said something of the sort to her. "Will you—will you be coming to the dance they're giving tonight?"

Charles hesitated.

"I'll try to get along for a while, but I think it's most unlikely that I'll manage it," he said at length. "Anyhow, I'll say goodbye now in case I can't."

He didn't come. All that evening Dinah waited expectantly, hoping at any moment to see his tall, commanding figure. But time swept remorselessly on until, at last, she had to accept it that he wasn't coming.

She went to bed that night with her mind in a state of bewilderment.

Of course it was disappointing that Charles hadn't come. It would have been nice to feel that one person present was a friend and not just a new acquaintance, however pleasant. Disappointing, yes. But surely of not such importance as to fill her with this aching sense of emptiness. It simply wasn't reasonable! After all, Charles had warned her that he might not be able to make it—

Charles had warned her! The phrase echoed in her mind and carefully she thought over all the other things that Charles had said that afternoon. Gradually she realised what it all added up to.

Charles making it very clear that the reason for his presence at the wedding was simply his relationship to Euan and was not in any way connected with the fact that she would be there as well.

Charles laying such emphasis, not once but twice, on the claims of his work.

And finally, Charles warning her, not in so many words, perhaps, but certainly by implication, that because he had come to her mother's and her aid in his professional capacity and would do again in similar circumstances she mustn't take it for granted that he was at her beck and call to dance attendance on her if they happened to meet on social occasions.

Charles, in other words, thinking that she was setting her cap at him was very firmly and unmistakably making it clear that he was not interested.

"And you really did enjoy yourself, darling?" the Contessa asked.

"Yes, I did," Dinah said firmly. "It was a beautiful wedding. Everything went so smoothly—that was due to Mrs. Joliffe, of course. The weather was perfect and Ellen looked lovely. Look—" she took some photographs from an envelope and handed them to her mother. "I took these with my little print-on-the-spot camera, and I got someone to take one of me because I thought you'd like it."

"I do, indeed," the Contessa agreed, studying the photographs intently. "Yes, Ellen did make a beautiful bride, and a very happy one. I've never met Euan, but he looks a likeable sort of person."

"He is," Dinah confirmed. "And he thinks the world of Ellen."

The Contessa smiled as she studied the next photograph—one of Mrs. Joliffe.

"Nina," she murmured affectionately. "How little she's changed. A little older, of course, but with just that same air of serenity that was there when we were both girls. How I should like to see her again!"

"Well, you can if you like," Dinah told her. "She asked me to say that she'd love to come and see you if it wouldn't be too much for you."

"Of course it wouldn't be," the Contessa replied eagerly. "It would be sheer delight. Will you write to her, Dinah? Tell her any time that would suit her."

"I'll tell her when I write to thank her for having me," Dinah promised. She gathered up the photographs. "Oh, Mother, such an odd thing happened," she went on casually. "Who do you think was at the wedding? But you'll never guess! Charles, of all people!"

"Charles?" There was no mistaking the Contessa's blank astonishment. "But how in the world did that happen?"

"He's distantly related to Euan," Dinah explained. "And I must say he looked extremely distinguished in morning dress!"

"Yes, it would suit him," the Contessa said absently. "But what an extraordinary coincidence!"

"Yes, wasn't it?" Dinah agreed, "It makes one feel like saying what a small world it is! And of course, the surprising thing really is that we didn't find out when Charles was here."

"Oh, I don't know," the Contessa said vaguely. "After all, it wasn't until after he'd left that we heard the wedding was to be sooner than originally planned. It was just something that was going to happen in the future, and so not particularly in our minds."

"Yes, of course," Dinah agreed with a feeling of relief. She still felt a little uneasy over Ellen's indiscretion. It was not that she resented the fact that Mrs. Joliffe had written to her mother in order to make sure that no unnecessary obstacles were put in the way

173

of her being Ellen's bridesmaid. None the less, even such kindly manoeuvring was a little disconcerting. Supposing something of the same sort accounted for Charles's reserved manner towards her? If someone had told him that she would be at the wedding in such a way that he detected at least a hint of matchmaking! No wonder he had been so unforthcoming!

Of course it was true that neither Ellen nor her mother appeared to know that she and Charles had met before, let alone in what circumstances, and that was reassuring. Now, her mother's surprise was so evidently genuine that Dinah came to the conclusion that it must, after all, have been sheer coincidence. And since she had no intention of going to England again in the near future, she could—and would—dismiss the whole matter from her mind.

CHAPTER TEN

A FEW days after Dinah's return, Guido left, promising to pay another visit, however brief, fairly soon. He said it very casually, but it was impossible not to know that he was anxious on his stepmother's account. Indeed, he said as much to Dinah.

"She is much better than I had anticipated. None the less, it is idle to pretend that a cure has been effected. You know that, Dinah?"

"Yes," Dinah said sadly, "I know."

"And you are not afraid to be here alone, except for the servants?" he asked, looking at her keenly.

"No," Dinah told him steadfastly, "I'm not afraid—and if I were, I'd stay just the same."

Guido patted her shoulder affectionately.

"You are very much like the little mother in some ways," he told her. "You give her the same loving loyalty that she gave my father."

He left shortly after, and Dinah missed him. Though there was no actual blood tie between them, she had not only grown fond of him, but had known that he felt the same way about her.

For a fortnight life resumed its earlier placid routine, with Dinah perhaps a little over-anxious on her mother's account. Surely she was not mistaken in thinking that the fragility which had always been evident had increased in the last weeks? She raised the point with Dr. Schwartz, who regretfully confirmed her fears.

"Yes, it is true, and, my child, there is nothing that can be done about it. It is nature taking its course. None the less, I am, at the moment, less concerned about the Contessa than I am about you."

"Me?" Dinah said in surprise. "But I'm quite well!"

"Up to a point, yes," Dr. Schwartz agreed. "But you have lost a considerable amount of weight since I first met you and you have also lost that splendid colour you had then. How often do you go out?"

"Not very often," Dinah confessed. "I really am quite busy, you know, and besides—" she bit her lip.

"It is very natural that you should want to be with your mother as much as possible," Dr. Schwartz nodded. "But do you not know that she is worried on your behalf —which is bad for her."

"I hadn't thought of that," Dinah acknowledged ruefully. "But I don't quite see how I can do anything about it—at least, not until Mrs. Joliffe comes next week."

"Next week," the doctor said approvingly. "Then we will say no more about it for the present, but I warn you, Fräulein Dinah, I shall keep my eye on you! And I shall expect to see the English roses blooming in your cheeks again! Do I make myself clear?"

Dinah agreed that he did and, in fact, she had already made up her mind that she would go out sometimes when Mrs. Joliffe arrived so that the two old friends could be alone together.

And her first trip, she decided, should be to the Tannenhof. Her clothes had been sent up from the hotel, but she had not been there since that terrible night when she and Charles and Nicky had battled their way up to the Chalet. There had been no reason why she should, but she had a feeling that until she did go back, the ghosts of the past could not be finally laid.

She telephoned Frau Emil to make sure that her visit would not be inconvenient, and being assured that she would be very welcome, accepted an invitation to afternoon tea.

It was strange to be in those once familiar surroundings, for it seemed to her that this was the first time she had ever been there.

"But of course it hasn't changed. It is I who have done that," she thought with a flash of insight as Frau Emil hurried out of the office to greet her.

"Lovely to see you!" she declared, slipping a friendly arm through Dinah's. "Come up to our sitting room."

It was a pleasant little meal and Frau Emil made

an ideal companion, for though she asked after the Contessa and Mrs. Joliffe whom she had met during an earlier visit, she didn't dwell on the subject. Nor, to Dinah's relief, did she make any reference to Nicky and the broken engagement. Instead, she discussed her own affairs, asking Dinah's opinion about new colour schemes for some of the bedrooms and telling her that they were thinking of building on to the hotel.

Then Emil, kind and friendly, came in and made Dinah feel doubly welcome. But he could only stay for a short time and almost as soon as he had gone, Frau Emil was called away.

"No, don't go," she said as Dinah showed signs of getting up. "I ought not to be long. Have a look at the magazines on that table. They're all in new today."

She was gone rather longer than she had anticipated and, after a while, Dinah began to glance through the magazines. They were all English of the glossy type and actually not of very great interest to her. The ones dealing with fashion she quickly disposed of, since she knew that she would never wear such exotic clothes. Nor, as she had neither house or garden of her own, did she spend much time on those dealing with such subjects. The remaining magazine dealt with social events and people, and this interested her more because she knew some of the people whose photographs appeared on its pages, particularly among those depicting newly married couples. She recognised two of the brides as she had met them at Ellen's wedding, as well as one of the bridegrooms. Then she turned the page—and caught her breath.

The whole page was given over to pictures of one wedding, and in this case, she had good reason to know both bride and groom.

Bébé Vallaise—and Nicky. Their faces smiled up at her, gay, confident and—happy? She studied them more intently. Most people would probably have said that they looked very happy indeed, but to Dinah's more perceptive eyes, another emotion predominated— triumph. Each of them had got what they wanted—no doubt about that. It was a look which, in Bébé's case,

177

was easy enough to interpret. She had wanted Nicky—and she had got him. It was as crude as that. But Nicky —Dinah frowned as she concentrated on the handsome face. Was she imagining it or, with the triumph, was another emotion blended? Anticipation—expectancy as if, though for the moment he was satisfied with the way things had turned out, this marriage was only the first step towards achieving his ambitions?

Yes, that was it! She remembered what Nicky himself had said about wanting a *real* job, and later, that his meeting with Mr. Vallaise was the chance of a lifetime. Still later, on the last occasion when they had been together, he had said that he had quite enjoyed the challenge of his trip to Dr. Schwartz's house that terrible night.

Challenge! Yes, that was what Nicky revelled in. She had realised it to some extent before, but now she seemed to see more clearly. Nicky *was* ambitious. He did want wealth and the power it brought, but he didn't want easy money, as she had tried to press on him. To give him real satisfaction, success must be founded on his own efforts—in taking up a challenge and coming out the victor! And that was why he had married Bébé. It gave him his opportunity to break into a world which had hitherto been closed to him. A ruthless, competitive world, but undeniably one in which there would be plenty of scope for a man like Nicky.

"I'm sorry I've been so long—"

Dinah started. She had been so absorbed in her thoughts that she had not heard Frau Emil come into the room.

"Oh, it's quite all right," she said hurriedly. "But I'm afraid I really must go now—"

But Frau Emil had taken the magazine from her and was gazing at the page which had riveted Dinah's attention with horrified eyes.

"My dear!" she exclaimed in dismay. "I'd no idea— I haven't had time to look at them! You must believe that because I'd never have let you—"

"Please don't worry," Dinah said earnestly. "Nicky

was quite free to do as he liked—and it was I who broke off the engagement, you know."

"That doesn't excuse—" Frau Emil began hotly, and stopped short. "It's not my business, I know," she went on slowly. "But I'm going to say this just once and then never again to anybody. I'm truly thankful, Dinah, that he has married that girl and not you! He just wasn't right for you!"

"And I just wasn't right for him," Dinah insisted. "I can see that now—and wonder how we could have made such a mistake. There's just nothing left. Truly, Frau Emil. And now I must go!"

And as she walked back to the Chalet, she knew that she had been right. She and Nicky had never really *belonged*. What was more, by visiting the hotel, she *had* laid the ghosts of the past, and if the means that had made that possible had been entirely fortuitous, what did that matter? It was the fact that was important. Nicky had gone out of her life for ever and his going had not even left a scar.

Mrs. Joliffe stayed for a fortnight and both the Contessa and Dinah missed her when she left. Her serenity was something which shone like a beacon, but there were other facets to her personality which were almost as endearing. She had the gift of appreciating other people's points of view and the willingness to fall in with their wishes. Without a word of explanation, she had understood Dinah's wish not to lay more emphasis on her mother's condition than was absolutely necessary. Yet, at the same time, she seemed to have an instinct for knowing when her old friend was tiring, and without fuss would quietly leave her to rest.

But best of all, it seemed to Dinah, was that listening to her mother and Mrs. Joliffe talking about the girlhood they had shared, she was able to piece together a picture of what her mother had been like in those early days. Gay, high-spirited, warmhearted, and above all, finding life an entrancing thing. And though, long since, Dinah had ceased to blame her mother in any way for leaving her father, this new knowledge set the seal on her belief. To such a girl, Esmond Sherwood's cold, unresponsive nature must have been sheer torture. No wonder that, at last, her resistance had been sapped away.

Very early one lovely summer morning about a month after Mrs. Joliffe had left, Greta came to Dinah's bedroom, and even before she spoke, Dinah knew what had happened. The Contessa had died very peacefully in her sleep.

Dinah went at once to her mother's room. It was the first time she had encountered death face to face, and that now she had, it should be someone as dear to her as her mother had become made it an awe-inspiring as well as a heartbreaking ordeal. Yet when she looked down at that sweet, tranquil face, fear left her, though the heartbreak remained.

After a few minutes she came out of the quiet room, but for a moment she leaned against the door she had just shut, her eyes closed. If only, at a time like this, one could be left in peace! But there was so much to do, and it was for her to do it. She must be businesslike and practical when every quivering, tormented nerve pleaded for solitude.

She forced herself to think coherently. She must let people know what had happened. She went to the telephone and made her first call to Dr. Schwartz, who promised to come to the Chalet at once. Then she called Guido's number. But it was Lucia who answered, her soft voice full of sympathy when she heard what had happened.

"Dear Dinah, I am so sad for you and for my dear Guido," she said gently. "But I am afraid you cannot speak to him. He flew to Germany last night on business, and though I know the name of the hotel where he is staying, I also know that he was leaving there very early this morning and where he will be going depends on the arrangements which the men he is meeting have made. I will, of course, telephone the hotel at once and make sure that he has a message as soon as possible. And I will also ring up his secretary in his office in case he should need to be in touch with her. I promise you I will do my best, dear Dinah, but—"

"Yes, I quite understand," Dinah assured her, though her heart sank. "Thank you, Lucia. Will you let me know if you do manage to get in touch with him?"

Lucia promised and Dinah rang off, but she didn't immediately lift her hand from the telephone.

"If ever you need me—if ever I can be of any use to you, let me know."

That was what Charles had said, and never in all her life had she wanted anything so much as she wanted his strong, comforting presence now. And he had meant what he had said. She knew that. Yet, in view of the way in which he had so unmistakably warned her that he was supremely lacking in any personal interest in her, how could she ask so much of him?

But even as she hesitated, the telephone bell rang, and when she lifted the receiver, incredibly, the one voice she longed to hear said crisply :

"The Chalet Farini? I want to speak to Miss Dinah Sherwood."

"Charles!" Dinah's voice shook uncontrollably.

"Dinah, what is it?" Charles asked urgently. "Your mother—?"

"Yes," Dinah said tremulously. "About an hour ago—"

"My dear!" He said no more than that, but there was a wealth of sympathy and understanding in his voice. "Are you alone? Your brother—?"

"He's away from home. He can't possibly be here before tomorrow at the earliest."

He didn't hesitate.

"Dinah, would it help if I flew out at once?"

"Oh, Charles! If only you could!" Dinah made no attempt to hide her longing for him.

"Right, then I'll get the earliest possible flight," Charles promised. "I'll be with you before evening. Goodbye until then, Dinah."

"Goodbye," she murmured, and waited for the click which meant that he had hung up before she herself rang off.

She felt bewildered and startled. Charles's unhesitating offer to keep his promise didn't surprise her. It was what one would expect of him. What was so incredible was that he should have rung her up at this precise moment. Another example of coincidence, or had he somehow been aware of her need? Thought transference? People said that there was such a thing, but surely only between two people who loved one another very much, not when only one of them cared.

So, much as she longed to know the truth of it, she knew that she must never embarrass Charles by asking why he had rung at that particular moment. Charles, she was quite sure, would never refer to the matter.

Charles reached the Chalet sooner than Dinah had dared to hope was possible. He had, he explained, been fortunate. A passenger had cancelled his reservation at the last moment and Charles had taken it over.

It seemed very right and natural for him to be here and for him to shoulder burdens which would otherwise have fallen on Dinah's, but he didn't make the mistake of doing so much that she had not enough to occupy her mind. And when everything possible had been done, he insisted that they should go for a walk together and would listen to no objections from her. Not that she put up much resistance. It was easier this way even though she knew that, sooner or later, she had got to face up to her loss in solitude. That was something which no one, not even Charles, could share.

But Charles, she discovered, had the gift of silence. Fully appreciating her need for human companionship, he was equally aware that this was a time when words were useless. Sympathy needed no speech to convey itself and the raw wound was too fresh for consolation to be possible.

So, in silence, they walked steadily for perhaps half an hour until, beside a small, impetuous waterfall, Charles pointed to an outcrop of rock and suggested that they should rest there for a while before making the return trip. Mechanically Dinah agreed, and once again they fell silent.

It was a very beautiful place to which he had brought her. From where they sat there was no sign of human habitation and except for the birds' evensong and the distant tinkling of cowbells, no sound disturbed them. They had it all to themselves—the green slopes they had climbed, the waterfall and, transcending all else, the majestic backcloth of the Alps. Green near at hand and individual, then, in the middle distance, blurring into a jagged outline until, in the far distance, they became a soft, misty purple.

At first Dinah was hardly aware of her surroundings, but gradually the peace of the place possessed her and she sighed deeply, wishing that time could stand still.

Charles, too, seemed content to stay and they sat on, each lost in their own thoughts and yet conscious of the presence of the other, until the shadows lengthened and a fresh little breeze warned them that it was time to go back.

That night, though she refused the sleeping draught which Charles suggested, Dinah slept deeply and dreamlessly as if, even in her sleep, Charles was standing between her and anything which could hurt her.

Guido arrived the next afternoon and from that moment there was a subtle change of atmosphere. For, though he accepted such arrangements as Charles had made without question, he naturally assumed authority now, and Charles, recognising his right to do so, quietly stepped down into second place—in more ways than one. Dinah couldn't fail to be aware that he felt it was for her stepbrother to give her the support and care she needed now—which let him out. True, he was always available if she asked anything of him, but how could she do that when, so unmistakably, it was a relief to him to be free of the responsibility of looking after her? The barrier was up again. Charles was kind and friendly, but not by the wildest stretch of imagination could she persuade herself that his interest in her went any deeper than that.

And if she needed further proof, she had it when, the day after the funeral, Charles said his farewells. In

183

the short time that they had known one another, the two men had clearly formed a liking for one another, and as they shook hands, Guido said heartily:

"I hope most sincerely that you will come and see us in Italy."

"That would be delightful," Charles replied pleasantly, but with such complete lack of enthusiasm that Dinah knew beyond doubt that he had no intention of doing anything of the sort.

Charles was going out of her life for good.

It was a relief to Dinah when the time came for her to leave the Chalet and go to Italy with Guido. For though her grief at losing her mother was too recent to be quickly assuaged, there were other memories which it might be easier to forget once she had left Alpenglühen. Not anything to do with Nicky. He already belonged to a past which seemed so unreal that it might never have happened to her at all. But Charles—that was different. At every turn she was reminded of those brief hours which they had spent together before Guido had come. Then, for a little while, and despite her grief, she had lived in a world that was full of the promise of happiness because she and Charles had seemed so close to one another. Now she knew that was just an illusion and must be forgotten. Perhaps in different surroundings and with new interests, she would find it easier.

Certainly everyone did their best to help her. With Guido she was already on easy terms and Lucia's welcome was reassuringly warm. But it was the children who, all unconsciously, helped her most. Little had been said in front of them about the Contessa's death, and their main preoccupation was the exciting arrival of a new sister who was not a squalling baby like other children's new sisters—and brothers, too, for that matter—but was grown up! For a while they were wary, keeping their distance. But that wore off quickly when they found that not only could Dinah swim like a fish in the garden pool, but that she had no silly ideas about such activities being dangerous for children as their *bambini* had. She would stand at the edge of the pool, clucking like a hen and wringing her hands in anticipation of imminent disaster. But Dinah taught them life-saving drill which they practised with such enthusiasm that they nearly succeeded in drowning one another.

So, one way and another, it seemed to Dinah that her mother had been right when she had said that this was a warmhearted little family circle which would gladly open to include her. That was, she felt, exactly what had happened.

And so the months wore away, sometimes with incredible speed, sometimes on leaden feet. She heard only very rarely from Charles, but that, she told herself stoically, was just as well. It gave her a better chance to forget him. It might even be better if he didn't write at all.

Then they were into December and at once Christmas became almost the sole topic of conversation, particularly where the children were concerned. It would, they assured Dinah excitedly, be the most wonderful day she had ever known. Willingly Dinah let herself be carried away on the wave of their enthusiasm. A family Christmas—something she had never experienced before. It was something to which she could look forward and she felt that she was succeeding in her determination to make a new life for herself.

Then, three days before Christmas, all her good resolutions were undermined and every scrap of her painfully built defences were battered down. The trouble began early in the day. Their mounting excitement had been too much for the children and they began to wrangle and quarrel. It all came to a head when Luigi gave Amelia's hair a vicious, painful tug to which she responded by bursting into tears and slapping her brother's face with sufficient force as to make him roar.

Fortunately Lucia was near at hand and quickly quelled the storm. But the children's *bambinia* came bustling in, breathlessly haranguing the children for their wickedness and loudly declaring that bed at once was the only fitting consequence to it. But that Lucia wouldn't have.

"No, Maria, that would do no good at all," she said firmly, above the din of the children's renewed clamour. "Instead, we will have a quiet little time together."

Dinah was out doing some last-minute shopping at the time, but she heard all about it from one of the maids as soon as she returned. The girl was obviously excited and delighted that, for once in a way, Maria had got her quietus, though Dinah thought that she was probably making too much of the incident on that account. As a result, when she had taken off her outdoor clothes and changed her shoes, she went downstairs to join them all without thinking very much about it. But at the half open door she paused. The only light came from the fire, the only sound, Lucia's soft voice telling an entrancing story. Smiling, Dinah, pushed the door a little further open—and stood rooted to the floor.

The maid had not told her that Guido had joined his family, but now the four of them were sharing the big sofa in front of the fire. Guido had Amelia cuddled in his arms, Luigi was snuggled up to his mother.

Dinah drew back silently and went up to her room. She locked the door and then she flung herself face down on the bed to weep the slow, burning tears of utter desolation.

With heartbreaking clarity she had known that it would have been an intrusion to go into that quiet room, for what she had seen had been a close-knit little group of people, complete in itself—a family which, though it might open its ranks generously to admit others less fortunate, had no need to.

Always, Dinah knew, she would receive love and kindness in her stepbrother's home, but she wasn't essential to their happiness. They had been complete without her, and would be again if she were to leave. She didn't really belong—she was an outsider—

As she always would be, unless a miracle happened which would make it possible for her to be at the very heart and core of just such another enchanted little circle.

Only such a miracle could never happen, because Charles didn't love her and never would.

She whispered his name over and over again and then, from the depths of her heart, a cry of longing welled up.

"Charles, Charles darling! I love you so much—how can I live without you?"

At last, when the children had almost given up hope, Christmas Day dawned. It wasn't easy to behave in a way which didn't cast a shadow over other people's happiness, but Dinah did her very best and if her smile was rather forced and she didn't talk much, no one seemed to notice in the general excitement. It was only at lunch time that Guido, looking first at his wife and then at Dinah, remarked that the pair of them looked completely exhausted.

"So," he announced, "as soon as we've finished this meal, I'm going to take the children off your hands so that you can both rest."

Lucia thanked him with a grateful smile and Dinah murmured something which was accepted as corroboration. But, in fact, the last thing she wanted was to be idle and so, when Guido went off with the children in the car and Lucia had gone upstairs to rest, she began to tidy up the inevitable litter of the day. Boxes, wrappings, ribbons were scattered all over the place and it was not until nearly an hour later that she felt satisfied with the result of her efforts. But restlessness still possessed her and she was glad that at that moment Guido returned with the children. Now she could occupy herself keeping her eye on them while Guido had a chance to relax. She went to the door, but at that moment it was opened a little and Guido spoke without coming in.

"Dinah, I've brought you a Christmas present, rather belatedly, but none the less one which you will welcome, I hope!"

The door swung wide and a man came in. Incredibly, it was Charles!

Dinah stood as still as if she had been turned to

stone. Charles was undeniably standing within a few feet of her, but why had he come? Why, why, *why*?

Their eyes met and Dinah had her answer as Charles held out his arms. Swift as a bird on the wing she flew to the welcome that awaited her.

"But, Charles darling, why didn't you tell me before?" Dinah asked him that evening.

Charles, blessing their tactfully absent host and hostess, drew her a little closer before he answered. They were sharing that same comfortable sofa in front of the fire, lost to everything but their own particular heaven.

"I was afraid to," he confessed.

"Afraid?" Dinah shrank a little into herself. "Because you thought that, having made a mistake once, I might do that same thing again?"

"No!" Charles denied emphatically. "Not that. Having had that experience, I don't believe you could fall into the same trap again."

"No, I don't think I could," Dinah mused. "If you've once mistaken tinsel for gold, you know the real thing for what it is. But if it wasn't that, why were you afraid?"

"Because it seemed possible—probable even—that though I knew that I loved you, I might so easily cause you the same unhappiness that your mother had known," and when she would have protested, he laid his finger gently over her lips. "No, you must listen, darling, because you've got to know what you're risking. You see, Dinah, your mother told me that your father was one of those men who should never have married, and I felt that she was right. But that didn't prevent me from understanding your father's absorption in his work because my own situation had always been the same. For years my driving force had been ambition. Not for the sake of money or prestige. It was *power* that I coveted. The power to be free to put my theories into practice with no one to gainsay me."

"But that was so that you could help people," Dinah said softly.

Charles shook his head.

"Don't tempt me to find excuses for myself, Dinah. I've done that for too long! But the truth is that my patients weren't so much people as laboratory specimens on whom I could try out my ideas. And it never occurred to me to question that point of view. Why should it? I succeeded where other men failed. But I paid a price for my ruthlessness. I lost, as your father lost, all sense of my own humanity and with it, all humility. I had no friends, and perhaps worse than that, I had no wish for them. I allowed myself no relaxation and so, finally, I came near to breaking point. That was when I decided to come to Alpenglühen to rest and recuperate. That, I thought, would be easy since no one knew me there—but I reckoned without fate! Almost immediately I became involved in the very personal affairs of someone else—a thing which I hadn't allowed to happen for many years. Your affairs. And do you know what my first impression of you was?" And when she shook her head: "That I had never seen anyone before who was so absolutely ecstatically happy."

"Yes, I was," Dinah said soberly. "But in a sort of fairy-tale way. It wasn't *real*."

"No, it wasn't," Charles agreed. "And I think I knew that immediately. What surprised me was that despite the fact that I subsequently found you to be a thorough nuisance, I also discovered that I hoped most sincerely that you would never become disillusioned."

"And that was when you knew you loved me?" Dinah asked.

"I might have known it, but I wouldn't admit it," Charles told her. "However, by the time your mother was taken ill, I couldn't deny it any longer, and with all my heart I wanted to help you."

"You did," Dinah said fervently.

"I was thankful to be able to," Charles said simply. "But of course, the fact that you turned to me then didn't mean that I thought you loved me. But when your engagement was broken, I was desperately tempted to tell you. But I held back. For one thing, you needed me to lean on, and if, as was more than likely, you turned me down, I knew you wouldn't feel that you could accept my help. Besides, by then I knew that your happiness meant more to me than my own, and seeing what sort of man I knew myself to be, how could I be sure that I could give it to you?"

"Yes, I see," Dinah said reflectively. "So, while you made it quite clear that if I needed your help, I'd only got to ask for it, in other ways you did your best to keep me at arm's length."

"Exactly," Charles said grimly. "It wasn't easy."

"No, it couldn't have been," Dinah agreed, but she sounded puzzled. "Charles, I do understand why you felt like that, but what's happened since to make you feel differently about it now? Because you do, or you wouldn't have come here now. So what's changed?"

"Well," he said slowly, "for one thing, I honestly believe I've got my priorities sorted out now. I know that human relationships are more important than success can ever be. And yet, strangely, I know I've done better work since I've realised that than I've ever done before." He was silent for a moment, then he went on deliberately: "There was something else as well—"

"Tell me," Dinah coaxed softly.

"You and I met by chance," he began slowly. "Well, what of it? People do make new acquaintances on holiday. Then we happened to meet at the wedding. Coincidence—but then coincidences do happen. But then something incredible happened. Do you remember when I rang you up that day? Didn't it strike you as strange that I should have done so at that particular moment?"

"Yes!" she said breathlessly. "It did. Do you know, my hand was actually on the telephone, but I couldn't quite find the courage to ring you up. Charles!" she turned to him eagerly. "Did you know? Was that why you rang?"

"I knew something like that," he admitted. "Quite suddenly I was absolutely sure that you were in trouble.

I told myself that I was letting my imagination run away with me. But I had to make sure."

"How wonderful!" Dinah breathed. "But why didn't you tell me?"

"It didn't seem possible that you could believe it—you might even not have wanted to," he explained. "Besides, there was, after all, a prosaic explanation. As a doctor I knew that your mother could only live a few months at the outside. You were constantly in my thoughts, so eventually I rang you up. That by chance I chose that particular moment I told myself could only be fortunate coincidence. What else could it be? Such a degree of rapport might be possible between two people who loved each other very deeply, but—"

"But not when, as you thought, it was only you," Dinah supplied eagerly. "But that's what I told myself, thinking it was only me! And we were both too blind to see—but that's not all, is it, Charles? There's something else!"

"Yes," he admitted deliberately. "There is! Two nights ago, I suddenly felt the same compelling conviction—you needed me! I had no choice but to come to you and find out why because, though such a thing happening once might be coincidence, for it to occur a second time meant something more than that. Dinah, was I right? Did you summon me? You did! Tell me, darling."

So, very simply, she told him just what had happened. Then, deeply moved by the experience they had shared, they fell silent until Charles held her from him and looked down into her tranquil, happy face.

"We belong to one another," he said almost sternly. "After this, there can be no doubt about it. And yet, Dinah, I'm still afraid for you. I've told you that I believe I've got my priorities sorted out. I know I have. None the less, mine is a demanding job which must frequently have first claim on my time, whether I want it that way or not. Will you be able to accept and tolerate that?"

Dinah put up her hand and tenderly caressed the

strong face as if to smooth away the anxiety which yet was so precious to her.

"Will you always want to come back to me?" she asked softly.

He drew her closer.

"That always, beloved!" he told her, his voice deepening to a passionate tender note that set her pulse racing. "Never doubt that!"

"Then I shall be able to wait and welcome you," Dinah whispered, and with a little sigh of contentment, surrendered her lips to his.

She would have to share him with those who needed his care and skill, but the knowledge brought no fear, for she knew that what he had said was true. Neither time nor distance could break the bond between them. Twice already they had proved that and so it would always be. Love such as they shared would always triumph.